To: Stevi

High Praise for "From the Ashes!"

"I intended to take a short break and read a few pages to get the story line in mind. Ha! I missed the evening news, the game shows; in fact, the whole evening because I couldn't put it down. The only things that slowed me down were supper and the many Kleenex moments. Bill Thomas has the gift of story telling that will capture and intrigue his readers. A must read."

– Will Hinton, Author of
The Rocky Mountain Odyssey series –

"Every good story is somehow a love story. In *From the Ashes*, first-time novelist Bill Thomas gives us once again the greatest Love Story of all – with an interesting new twist. Enjoy!"

– Mary Mueller, Author of
The Redemption of Matthew Ryersen –

"*From the Ashes* is a touching story of love and redemption. Bill Thomas has penned an impressive work of fiction."

– RG Yoho, Author of
The Kellen Malone Western series –

"*From the Ashes* is a great debut from page one. An emotional roller coaster, this is a book that tugs at your heart and refuses to let go."

– Josh Clark, author of
The McGurney Chronicles series
and Dakota Divided –

Cover design created by Ron Bell of AdVision Design Group (www.advisiondesigngroup.com)

ISBN 978-1-61808-021-9

Printed in the United States of America

White Feather Press

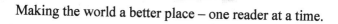

Making the world a better place – one reader at a time.

Bill

Thomas

From the Ashes

A Story of Redemption

Acknowledgements

Writing this story has been a joy for me, but it was a long process. There are quite a few folks that helped bring it to life along the way and I want to thank them for doing so.

I am indebted to Skip Coryell and White Feather Press for believing in this story and making possible what you now read. Throughout this process you have shown great patience, encouraged me, and given me insight into what it means to be an author. From reworking the title, designing the cover and writing the back copy, you have been outstanding. I appreciate the values White Feather Press promotes and I'm honored to be a member of the family.

I want to thank my editor, Mary Mueller. Your work on this story was brilliant. Your careful edits taught me not only how to write a better manuscript, but how to tell a better story. The words are not nearly adequate, but thank you.

I need to thank some good friends who worked with me to help make this story as clean and crisp as it can be. Kelsey Curran, Lucas Sweitzer and Kari Hoyes did excellent work proofreading and cleaning up my errors. Kristy Mader, Tonya Cannon, Diana Whittington and Ladonna Sweitzer read the story at various times and were encouraging. Traci Storie helped me greatly with formatting the manuscript and other computer issues. TeAnne Chartrau has been great with pictures and setting up a webpage.

I also want to thank Kimber Lane. A discussion you and I had was the genesis for this story. I don't know if the story exists without your input.

I also want to thank you, the reader. Thanks for buying the book. I hope you like it.

From the Ashes

Chapter One

It was unseasonably warm for a September morning in Cincinnati. The Reds were playing out their string of games once again with no chance at the playoffs, and the Bengals were off to a slow start with a rookie quarterback from Ohio State. Disputes between the unions and state officials had calmed a bit, so there wasn't really a lot of excitement on the bank of the Ohio River. Traffic on 75 into downtown was heavy, even for a Monday, but Jerold Volker wasn't fazed by the traffic. He was quite content on his drive to work.

"That's right," he said into his cell phone, "Fax that loan proposal this afternoon. Sure. We'll check it out today. Thanks."

He ended the call and drove his BMW along the highway toward the downtown exit. Jerold worked at one of the oldest and most prestigious banks in Ohio, where his promotion to vice-president six months earlier had caused quite a stir. It had been a long time since someone that young had reached such a high position. For Jerold, however, it was not a surprise. Success was his destination and he had come far on that journey. The 2009 BMW was a reward he'd given himself for the promotion. Tailored suits and designer sunglasses were his style. He was proud of what he'd accomplished and didn't mind if people knew it.

He eased the BMW into his assigned parking space, replaced some of the paper work that had spilled from the stack of folders he had taken home and walked quickly to the door.

"Good morning, Ed," Jerold called out to the security guard at the desk.

Ed Payne, a recently retired veteran of the police force and now full-time security guard, stood behind the desk at the basement entrance to the bank. He was an older man, a little thinner and grayer on top, but still as strong as he had been when he patrolled the streets of the Queen City. As the leader of the security team, Ed took seriously protecting the bank and its employees. He pushed the sign-in sheet toward the young man.

"Sign in, Jerold. I know it's a hassle, but no exceptions. Can't be too careful; there are a lot of nuts out there."

"Okay, Ed. It seems like a waste of time to me and a lot of work for you, but I'll do it."

Jerold signed the top line of the day's sign-in paper and slipped it back to Ed.

"Thanks, Jerold. Have a good day."

As he walked away, Jerold called back, "Thanks, you have a good one, too, Ed."

Jerold walked to the first floor elevator, where a dozen other employees huddled, who, like Jerold, had arrived early. The bank seemed to draw those who were ambitious. None of them, though, would ride to the eighteenth floor where his office was, where the power was.

Finally, the light flashed on the eighteen. The elevator opened and Jerold stepped out to a plush office area. He smiled as he passed the offices of the other vice presidents, still empty and dark. Once again, he was first. His office was at the end of the long hallway, guarded by a smaller office belonging to his secretary, Patrisse McKenzie. She wasn't in yet, so Jerold passed by her empty desk and entered his sanctuary. He took off his jacket and sat at the mahogany desk. For just a moment, he thought of all that had happened to him in the last couple of years. An MBA from Duke University had opened quite a few doors. A lot of his fellow classmates and professors had been surprised that he went back to the Midwest when an East Coast financial power seemed to be an ideal fit. Many guessed he'd decided to go home.

Jerold hadn't exactly come home, but Cincinnati was close to where he was from and he knew the city well. It didn't take long to begin the climb up the ladder. Jerold made few friends along the way, but that didn't really matter; friendships were secondary. Success was all that mattered. Now his moment of reflection was interrupted by the arrival of his efficient, but loud, secretary.

"Patrisse. It's about time," Jerold said a bit sarcastically as he stepped to the door of his office.

"I'm still twenty minutes early," she shot back at her young boss as she slid the tray holding two coffee cups onto the desk. "I know you didn't eat this morning, so I brought you a fruit salad from the grocer down the street and some coffee. You don't have to thank me, just eat."

He and Patrisse had been together for most of his career at the bank. A fantastic secretary who could get out paper work in no time, Patrisse had a knack for determining which calls were important and which were a waste of time. She ran interference better than any lineman on the Bengals' roster. She was never at a loss for words, either. No topic was out of her realm. There were times when this irritated Jerold, but not always, especially when she was talking about Darrion.

Darrion was ten years old and Patrisse's only child. His father had abandoned them when Darrion was only a baby, and Patrisse was a good mother, though not very confident in her abilities. Being a single mom was tough, even for a strong woman like Patrisse. Jerold admired her, but would never tell her so. His opinions and affirmations mattered to her and she would often seek out his thoughts about Darrion. It was a good work relationship; the best as far as Jerold was concerned. However, Patrisse did, from time to time, nag him with her concerns about his personal life. She would pester him about meeting with his sister or chide him about his dating life and his inability to commit to anyone. They worked long hours together and had many conversations.

"Thank you, Patrisse," Jerold said as he took the sack and a cup of coffee. "How was your weekend? How did Darrion do at his game?"

Patrisse smiled and sat down. She turned on her computer and took a sip of coffee.

"It was fine. Darrion had a great time. They lost twenty to eight. He scored a touchdown, though."

"That's awesome! He's a great player."

Patrisse looked up at Jerold as she spoke, "He wanted to know if you could come to one of his games. Do you think you can?"

Jerold grinned slightly and replied, "I'll see what I can do. Let's get to work. What do you have on the Brackman file?"

The work day began for everyone on the eighteenth floor and throughout the building. Deals were discussed and made. Transactions were completed and the bottom line got better. Even in slow economic times, there was money to be made, and Jerold Volker was in his element. He was one of the best. Noon seemed to come rather quickly, and it was an interruption to Jerold.

As he was analyzing a new proposal, his intercom buzzed.

"Mr. Volker," Patrisse's voice came from the speaker, "I'm breaking for lunch. Are you? I know. I know. I'll bring you something from Soakie's Deli. I'll be back before one."

Patrisse left and Jerold went back to work, immersing himself in the numbers of a potential merger in the New England states. His personal cell phone buzzed, but he was too busy to get it. Since it was just a text message, he'd get it later.

When Patrisse returned, she forced Jerold to take five minutes to eat. He quickly ate a turkey sub and drank a bottle of water, thinking that he didn't take care of himself very well, but at least he abused himself in a healthy way.

"Patrisse, while you were gone, I was able to crunch

the numbers and figure out how that deal in Baltimore can work for us. When you can, get those numbers out and up to Lonaker. I left the papers for you in your file."

"Wonderful," she answered, matching his earlier sarcasm.

Though she would always banter with him, inwardly she marveled at this young man's talent and his drive. He could be president of this institution some day. Still, though, she worried about him. He was young, talented and ambitious. He had everything going for him. What he didn't have many of, though, were friends. Sure, he knew a lot of people, but he had no real relationships. He dated plenty, but nothing of any substance. She knew that something wasn't quite right. She had tried many times to have a "big sister/little brother" talk with him, but it never worked. Whenever she got close to something significant, he just made a joke and laughed it off. One day she intended to really talk to him. That one day, however, would not be today.

"Let's get back at it," Jerold said as he quickly drained the bottle of water.

The rest of the day went by as quickly as the first half and soon Jerold had completed another profitable day for the company and for himself.

"Mr. Volker," Patrisse's voice came across his intercom, "I've completed the spreadsheet for the Baltimore folks and put it back in your file. It's ready to go upstairs. It's after five and I need to pick up Darrion. Is there anything else you need from me?"

Jerold answered, "No, I think that's it for today. Have

a good evening, Patrisse. Tell Darrion I said 'hey.'"

Jerold marveled at the way Patrisse worked so hard and was so dedicated to her job and to her son. He knew what her evening would be like: Get Darrion, go home, and prepare dinner. They would do homework together and then she would put Darrion to bed. Thirty minutes would be hers before exhaustion set in. She would sleep for a little while and then get up early and do it all over again. He was impressed with her work ethic.

His evening would be somewhat different. A glance at his watch told him it was five forty-five and he had a dinner date with Darcy. Patrisse hadn't mentioned it before she left, but he knew she was aware of it. He was sure Darcy had called sometime during the day. She and Patrisse talked a lot.

Jerold had been seeing Darcy for almost a year. He had dated a lot of different women over the years, but had never settled down with one. He had come close once, just after he graduated with his undergraduate degree. Her name was Ann and they talked of marriage and a family, but graduate school proved to be a stronger suitor. Jerold broke it off and Ann went back to Colorado. Since then, Jerold had dated some, but never with the intent of anything serious. He had met Darcy at a Christmas party. She was a high school counselor and a friend of a friend, and he was instantly attracted to her. She liked sports as he did and they bought season tickets to both the Reds and Bengals games. She had cultured tastes, too; she liked the theater and the art museum, and they shared a passion for jazz. They had seen each other regularly for quite a while now, and lately she'd been saying she loved him. Jerold wasn't sure what that might mean, but he was certain he wasn't going to say it.

Jerold grimaced. "I've got about forty-five minutes until I've got to get Darce," he said to no one in particular. "I guess this proposal will wait."

He stacked the petroleum company's papers and put them in the folder, to get his full attention first thing in the morning. He took his jacket from the old fashioned coat tree in the corner of his office and slipped it on as he walked out of the door. The eighteenth floor offices were nearly vacant as Jerold made his way to the elevator, where the doors opened on an empty car. The bell clanged for the basement level, and as he got off, he saw the night security guard, Jason.

Jason Gorman was a part of Ed's security team and as serious about the job as Ed was. That, though, was the only similarity. Jason was a young man from Kentucky whose goal was to get into the police academy. He didn't have the toughness of a seasoned law enforcement officer, at least not yet, but he admired Ed and was trying to learn from him.

"Howdy, Mr. Volker," he called out as he saw Jerold coming down the hall. "I see you stayed late again tonight."

"Yeah, Jason. It's like my father said, 'You gotta work to eat.' I like to eat and apparently you do, too."

He added that last remark as he patted Jason's rather large belly and Jason laughed.

"You've got that right!"

Jerold chuckled all the way to his car. Still several feet away from the BMW, he got out his keys to open the door. As he reached into his pocket, he also felt his cell phone. In the car, he looked at the phone, which showed one text message. The engine roared to life and he shifted into reverse as he checked the text. Jerold glanced at it quickly and then put the car back into park. The message was weird and it unnerved him. There was no name connected to it, and the number from which it came was listed as "unknown." What was really disturbing, though, was the message itself:

Help Me.

Jerold dropped the phone down onto the passenger seat next to him. It had to be a prank. No doubt. Right away he started thinking of everyone who might have done it. Craig in Accounts Payable was a suspect; this was definitely his kind of humor. Ryan and Dave in Human Resources might have had a part in it. They would love it if "old Jerold" was sent off on a wild goose chase. He was certain they would want to embarrass him. The more he thought about it, though, the more he was bothered. If it was someone at work, wouldn't that number show up on the message? How could they have made it "unknown?" Why would they just send a message, "Help me?" There wasn't anything really funny about that. His mind was consumed with the short message, and in no time he was at Darcy's condo. He parked the BMW and walked to her front door, where he had barely knocked before Darcy opened the door.

"Hey, Jer, you're on time tonight. Was it a slow day at work?"

Normally her jab would have elicited a response from Jerold. He never missed an opportunity to verbally joust.

Tonight, though, he was preoccupied.

"Hey, Darce, are you ready? Let's go."

Darcy found his demeanor strange and told him so as she got into the car.

"What's wrong, Jerold? Did something happen at work?"

Jerold furrowed his brow as he backed the car out of the parking spot and eased down the drive.

"Oh, it's probably nothing, Darce. It's really nothing."

Though he said it as calmly as he could, Darcy was unconvinced.

"Come on, Jerold, what's wrong? I can tell it's something. I want to know. Tell me."

Jerold sighed and drove south on I-75 to their favorite out-of-the-way restaurant.

"Okay," he finally relented. "I got this text message today and I can't figure it out. Look at it--" he handed her the phone-- "Strange isn't it?"

Darcy took the phone and read the message, and then she sat quietly for what seemed like several minutes.

"Who would do this?" she finally asked.

"Hey, I don't know," Jerold shot back, becoming more than a little agitated. "If I knew, then it wouldn't be a problem, would it?"

"I know," Darcy replied, trying to defuse the situation. "I just meant who would have done this and what does it mean? It's so strange. That's all."

Jerold didn't say anything else as he drove. Darcy, too, was lost in thought.

At the restaurant, they sat at a familiar table and

scanned the menu mindlessly. Normally a meal at this restaurant was nice for both of them, but tonight it was not such a good time. Darcy broke the awkward silence.

"Have you asked Patrisse about this?"

Jerold shook his head.

"No. I didn't check it until after she left."

"Let me see it again," Darcy said as she took the phone from him. "Okay. The text came in just after noon today. Do you remember it?"

Jerold thought for a moment.

"Yeah, I do. I mean, kind of. I was really busy at lunch today. Patrisse went out to Soakie's for lunch. I'll bet that's it! I'll bet she texted me from the deli. I'll talk to her about it tomorrow. I'm sure that's it. When she got back, she already had all she needed and didn't mention it. I never checked it, so I didn't ask about it. I'm sure that's what happened."

Darcy smiled and picked up her fork.

"I'm sure you're right, Jer. Let's have dinner now, okay?"

Jerold relaxed for the first time since he'd left the bank. He would talk to Patrisse tomorrow. That would settle this strange episode. The waiter brought their food, and for the next couple of hours, Jerold did not think any more about text messages.

Chapter Two

Jerold dropped Darcy off at her condo and then drove home. He seemed to be on auto pilot as he pulled the BMW into his covered parking space. He unlocked the front door of his expensive apartment and tentatively scanned the dark room, unnerved that he was, well, afraid. He had not been afraid of the dark for a long time. More apprehensive than he would ever admit, he groped for the light switch and was relieved to find it. The light brightened the room and lightened his mood. He went to his bedroom and hung his coat on the suit hanger. Then, more settled than before, he loosened his tie and hung it in the closet. In just a few moments Jerold went from a well-dressed professional to a thirty-something man in the suburbs dressed in basketball shorts and a t-shirt. He usually went right to bed after a full day and a busy night, but that wasn't going to happen tonight. Though the issue had been resolved, at least as to what he could do, he couldn't seem to stop thinking. The bedroom television provided no relief; after a couple of hours of mindless reruns, he was still awake.

Exasperated, he went to the living room and turned on some jazz. Though the music was soothing, Jerold spent a rough night in his leather recliner, unable to get that strange, two-word text message out of his mind. He kept telling himself it was ridiculous and no reason to lose sleep, but he couldn't relax. The alarm buzzed, echoing through the apartment as he got up slowly from the chair. Jerold stumbled into the dark bedroom, clicked off the alarm and trudged to the shower, determined to find out what was going on before he did anything else. As he showered, he scolded himself for being such a wimp. That text was a silly, stupid thing that didn't make any difference at all. He laughed at himself and concluded that by noon today he would have an answer and regret the hours of sleep he'd lost over something so foolish.

It was still dark when he pulled the BMW out of his parking space. The streets of Cincinnati were not yet filled with rush-hour traffic, so Jerold had the highway to himself as he sped toward downtown. He put his cell phone down in the passenger seat next to him, because he didn't seem to want it in his pocket. Every now and then he stole a glance at it, as if it might betray him again somehow. For the ten minutes it took to get from his complex to downtown, though, the phone remained silent. As he pulled into his parking space in the empty garage, he shook his head.

"Man, Jerold, you're losing it," he said aloud to no one but himself. "Get a grip."

He picked up the file folder containing the petroleum company proposal, stashed his cell phone in his pocket and walked quickly across the garage.

I just need a good day at work. That's what will clear my head, he thought as he punched in the building code. Jason was still at the security desk. It was too early for Ed's shift.

"Wow Mr. Volker, you're in really early today. I haven't even clocked out yet!"

"I know, Jason, I know, but like my dad said when I was growing up, 'Working hard is good for what ails you.'"

Jason was puzzled and asked, "You okay, Mr. Volker? You aren't ailing, are you?"

Jerold shook his head.

"No, Jason, I'm fine. That's just an expression."

"Oh, okay," Jason replied as he buzzed Jerold into the building. "Have a good day, sir."

Jerold walked the basement hallway to the elevator. There wasn't a soul in sight; he really was in early. When he pushed the button on the elevator, the doors opened immediately; and when he pushed the eighteen, the elevator rose quickly, without stopping, to the eighteenth floor, where Jerold stepped out into a dark and abandoned room. Walking through the dark office made Jerold as uneasy as he had been the night before. Again, he felt foolish, until the end of the hall brought relief and familiarity. Finding the light for Patrisse's office, Jerold clicked it on. Her desk was empty, of course; she wasn't in yet, and no one else was either. He moved quickly past her desk and opened the door of his own office. After stepping inside, he began to breathe a bit easier. It was strange. He hadn't been afraid of the dark since he was a small boy; now, though, those old fears seemed to be back.

His own office and routine brought him peace as he sat down at his desk and logged into his computer. *It may be only five here, but in Europe it is time for business*. With that thought and only that thought in mind, Jerold Volker began his work day. By the time Patrisse arrived, Jerold was immersed in product lines from a company in Baltimore. She peeked in his door and nodded to him as he spoke on the phone. He waved at her and gestured something, but she couldn't make it out. She simply smiled and held up a cup of steaming coffee and returned to her desk. In a few minutes Jerold came out.

"Good morning, Mr. Volker," Patrisse said, smiling.

"Where have you been? I've been waiting for you!"

Patrisse was somewhat taken aback by his abruptness, but she had seen it before.

"Well, let me guess who got up on the grumpy side today. Didn't you and Darcy have a nice time last night?"

Jerold grimaced and replied, "I'm sorry, Patrisse. It's just that, well, I wanted to check something with you."

"What is it?"

Though Jerold had waited for this moment for almost twelve hours, he was at a loss how to tell his secretary that he was acting weird about some silly text message.

"I'm waiting," Patrisse broke the silence. "You know time's money."

Jerold decided just to tell her the straight truth.

"Patrisse, I got a text message yesterday about noon. You didn't happen to send one to me while you were at

Soakie's, did you?"

Jerold was hoping more than anything that her answer was "yes." Then he could make fun of himself for being a big baby and let it go. It seemed to take forever for Patrisse to answer.

"No, I didn't send you any text messages yesterday."

Jerold dropped his head noticeably.

"Why do you ask? Jerold, what's the matter? What did it say?"

Jerold no longer tried to hide his frustration. He pulled out his cell phone, opened it and thrust it at her.

"You read it."

Patrisse clicked on the text messages. It came up quickly. She looked at it and then looked to Jerold. She looked at it again and then to Jerold once more.

"I don't get it," she finally said. "What does it mean?"

"I don't know," Jerold said angrily, "but I intend to know."

There wasn't much time to find out that morning. Patrisse's intercom buzzed. The secretary of the company president Derek Lonaker said Jerold needed to meet with Derek right away concerning the Baltimore project. Jerold gathered the file, waved to Patrisse and headed for the twentieth floor. The meeting with Lonaker, about the project and a few other proposals, took up most of the morning, and it was nearly noon when he returned.

"Is everything okay?" Patrisse asked.

"Yeah, the meeting was fine. He's hoping we can squeeze a little more from them, but we're just about ready to close that one."

Patrisse started, "What about the text?"

Jerold knew what she was thinking. Before she could finish he replied, "Haven't heard anything."

Patrisse nodded and sat down in her chair. Jerold stood at her desk for just a moment. The silence was a bit awkward. Jerold broke it.

"Hey, I think we're being crazy about this thing. It was a text message from some kid pranking a random number. There's nothing more to it. I'm sure that's all it is. Let's get back to work."

Patrisee nodded and said, "You're right. It was so strange. We'll let it go."

She then noticed the clock on the wall.

"It's almost noon; you want to get something at Soakie's or that new place downtown?"

"No. You go, Patrisse. Bring me something back. I want to get busy working."

Patrisse frowned a bit, but picked up her purse and left the office area for the elevator. Jerold went back to his office and sat at his desk. Again, he felt safe here. He awoke his computer and began tinkering with the numbers for the Baltimore project. About a half an hour or so later, his cell phone buzzed, not a call, but a text message. Jerold froze at the computer, and then reached for his phone. The face flashed the word "Text." He took a deep breath and pushed the button to retrieve it. He knew it almost before he finished reading. There was no number and no identification as to where the text originated. The message was direct:

Please. Help me.

Jerold placed the phone on his desk and stared into

the computer screen. A wide range of emotions built up inside of him-- Anger and frustration were joined by curiosity and bewilderment. He couldn't imagine who was messing with him.

Patrisse came back from Soakie's with a bag for Jerold, but he was already hard at work. She opened the door to his office to find him in a rather heated phone conversation.

"No, Craig, I'm not accusing you of anything. I just want to know who is doing it."

Patrisse could hear an angry Craig on the other end vehemently denying whatever accusation Jerold was making. Jerold apologized and then hung up the phone.

"What's going on?" Patrisse asked.

Angrily, Jerold picked up his cell phone and handed it to her. "Just this," he told her, his frustration building.

"Another one," Patrisse said.

"Read it," Jerold shot back.

Patrisse read it and shook her head.

"I don't think this is a prank or a game, Jerold."

"I don't either. I've already confronted Craig and the guys at Accounts Payable. They don't know anything about it and they don't appreciate being accused of stuff, either."

"Who might be trying to contact you? I mean, really. Who might want to get a hold of you?"

"You didn't give Darrion my number, did you? He wouldn't be messing around with me?"

Now Patrisse was somewhat offended by Jerold's accusation.

"No, I didn't. Darrion wouldn't do it, even as a

joke."

Jerold quickly calmed.

"I'm sorry, Patrisse. I know Darrion wouldn't do that. You don't think he's in some kind of trouble, do you?"

Patrisse thought about it for a moment.

"I don't think so, but I'll talk to him."

"Will you do me a favor? Call him at school right now. Make sure he's all right."

Patrisse frowned, but she agreed. She wanted to make sure for herself now as much as for Jerold. He followed her to her desk and waited as she dialed the number. It was a strange request, but she asked to speak to her son. Fortunately, the school secretary knew Patrisse from school events, and in no time at all she was speaking to Darrion. Jerold heard only her side of the conversation.

"How are you, honey?"

"Good, good. I'm glad," she answered to whatever Darrion said.

"Listen, you don't have Mr. Volker's cell phone number, do you? You haven't tried to call him or text him lately? Oh, I don't know. No reason. Thank you, dear. Have a good rest of the day. I'll see you when I pick you up tonight. Yes. We'll have tacos."

She hung up the phone.

"He said he doesn't have your number. He hasn't called, Jerold."

Jerold sat down at the chair by Patrisse's desk. He looked lost.

"What am I going to do?" he finally asked her.

"Have you called Darcy? Maybe she can help. She is a counselor." Before she could finish, Jerold cut her off. "I'm not crazy," he snapped at her. "This is just too weird."

"Let me call her and see if there isn't something we can do to trace these kinds of calls or text messages. I don't know much about them, but I bet she does. High school kids use this stuff all the time. If anyone knows how to find out who's behind it, I bet she can help."

Jerold agreed and Patrisse called Darcy's school. When Jerold told her about the latest message, she asked for his phone service company, got all of his information and said she would try to get some answers for him by the end of the day. Jerold hung up the phone and sat down in the chair by Patrisse's desk.

"I just don't get it. Why is this happening to me? What does it all mean?"

Patrisse didn't have any answers. She just listened.

"Patrisse, what do you think?" he asked her. "Am I going crazy, or is this some kind of, I don't know, test or something?"

Patrisse swallowed hard. What she was about to say, she had never said to him, but it seemed right to say it now.

"Jerold," she began tentatively, "have you prayed about this? Have you tried to give this to the Lord? Maybe you should."

He looked at her with a mixture of surprise and skepticism.

"Look Patrisse, I know you're a church-goer. You believe in Jesus, and I'm not against it. You know that. I just never really had much time for it. It's just not for me."

She accepted his answer for the time being.

"Okay, I'll just pray for you myself."

"All right. Do what you think is best," Jerold replied as he stood. "We had better get back to work. Darcy will have something for us by the end of the day. We'll know pretty soon who is harassing me and then we'll figure out what to do about it."

Jerold went back to his office and spent time behind his computer, but he didn't focus much on his work. His mind kept wandering. He wondered just what was going on. He couldn't get Patrisse's words out of his mind, either.

Pray about it. He'd heard that before and it didn't work. No. He wasn't about to pray for anything. His thoughts were interrupted by the squawking of the intercom on his desk.

"Jerold," Patrisse's voice announced, "you have a call on line one. It's Darcy."

"Thanks," Jerold answered.

He picked up the phone, "Hello, Darce. What did you find out?"

As he spoke, Patrisse came in quietly and stood by his desk. Jerold just stood with the phone to his ear. He would utter an occasional "yeah" or "uh huh."

"Thanks," he said at the end of a few minutes. "I'll get back with you. I will. I promise."

He hung up the phone and looked at Patrisse. She spoke first.

"Well, what did she find out? Anything?"

Jerold looked down and then answered, "Yeah, she contacted some folks who were able to use my information to trace where the call came from."

"And what did they say?"

"It came from a small town in western Kentucky called Pikesville."

Patrisse was really puzzled now.

"Pikesville, I've never heard of it. What's that?"

"It's a small town in the middle of nowhere, Kentucky. There can't be more than a couple hundred people living there."

"How do you know that?"

"I grew up there."

Chapter Three

*P*atrisse didn't say anything for a while. What was there to say? Jerold just stood at his desk. Finally, after a few minutes, Patrisse spoke.

"What does that mean? Why are you getting these messages from your old hometown?"

Jerold cleared his throat and replied, "I don't know who could be sending them. I haven't been to Pikesville in almost twenty years. When I left there after high school there wasn't much town left. I can't imagine that there's anyone there now."

Patrisse offered a few more comments and guesses as to what might be happening. She had plenty to say and Jerold heard, but he wasn't really listening. His mind was back in Pikesville twenty years ago, seeing it as if it were only yesterday...

Main Street in Pikesville was where the action was, at least as much action as ever happened in places like Pikesville. There was a Quik Mart on Main, and opposite that was a Burger Barn. A local pizza place was on Third Street. On the other side of Third was a Dari

Ring. Those four places formed the square in which the fun times took place. Jerold, in his mind's eye, could see Miller's Drug Store. Old man Miller, the owner, had given Jerold his first job. Making deliveries and stocking were the source of his first paycheck.

Not far down the street from the Dari Ring was the Baptist church, and now it was as if Jerold were walking that street. Next to the church was a cemetery, but Jerold did not linger there. At the end of Main Street was the Pikesville School. As in many American small towns, the school was consolidated. All kids, from kindergarten through high school, went to the same building. On one side of the school building was a playground. Swings, tunnel slides and merry-go-rounds dotted that part of the school grounds, and on the other side was a football field with some rotting wooden bleachers, two on the home team side and one on the visitors' side. Slightly crooked goal posts stood like scarecrows on each end of the field. It was on that cow pasture turned gridiron that Jerold Volker had excelled. The Pikesville Pirates had been, for Jerold's three years of playing, an eight-man football power in Kentucky. They reached the playoffs through-out his high school career and won a state champion-ship. The banner hung in the school gym, a source of pride for Pikesville. In many ways, it was the only thing Pikesville had of which they could be proud.

Pikesville, like many small towns, was dying. Young people were leaving Pikesville upon graduation to seek more opportunities and greener pastures. It hadn't always been like that. At one time, Pikesville was set to become an industrial town and an attractive place for families. A big factory had bought up land on the east side and jobs were going to be plentiful. After a few years, though, things got hard. The factory closed down, people left, and all that was left behind was a little farming community. The hopes and dreams of Pikesville dried up in the hot Kentucky sun. The little farming town was becoming a ghost town by the time Jerold graduated. He felt no remorse whatsoever for joining those who fled. He had bigger and better things ahead than what Pikesville could offer.

Not far from the school was Cambridge Street. Cambridge Street was a dead end, not a cul-de-sac, but a dead end, with a row of houses on each side. There were some nice homes in Pikesville, and a few big farms. None of them, though, was on Cambridge Street. These were small, cookie-cutter houses, built a long time ago for workers at the factory. They had been good starter homes, once. In Jerold's day, however, they became refuge for those who couldn't afford much else. Jerold's mind ambled down Cambridge Street until he reached 203. Abruptly, he stopped. He was jolted back into the present by Patrisse's insistence…

"Don't you agree, Jerold?" she demanded.

He couldn't hide that he had no idea what she was talking about, so he simply acknowledged it.

"I'm sorry, Patrisse. I haven't been listening. What did you say?"

"I said, I think you need to get with Darcy and track this down. Something must be going on in Pikesville and I believe you should find out what. Have her make some calls or you make them. Do something."

Jerold thought about what she suggested. He wasn't sure he wanted to involve Darcy, but he was curious as to what was going on in Pikesville. It had been so long and, while he had no desire to go back, something seemed to be drawing him.

"I'll talk to her tonight about it."

"Good, I'm glad. I'm going to keep praying, too. I want you to know that. Tomorrow night is our Bible study. I'll mention it there. You can come, if you want."

"You just keep on praying. I'll think about that Bible study. Now, let's finish up something productive today before we get fired."

Patrisse returned to her desk, knowing that there was no way Jerold was going to Bible study. He probably didn't want her prayers, either, though he was too polite to say it. She decided she would pray anyway. She would tell Darrion to pray, too.

Jerold went back to work and, for a few hours, he occupied his mind with the thoughts of acquisitions and potential mergers. It was about five-thirty or so when Patrisse buzzed him to tell him she was leaving. She reminded him to call Darcy.

About a half hour later, Jerold turned off his computer and gathered his papers. He called Darcy, who was anxious to hear from him.

"Hey Darce," he said as she picked up the phone. "How was your day?"

"Come on, Jer," she shot back. "Don't be silly. What matters is what is happening with you. What are you thinking about those strange texts?"

"I'm not sure, Darce, but I think I'd like to talk about it over dinner. Can you be ready in half an hour? We'll go to down to Florence; our place. I don't want to be around a big crowd tonight."

"Sure, I'll be ready."

Jerold hung up the phone. He picked up a few random folders and walked down the hall to the elevator where he ran into Marc Hernandez.

"Hey Jerold, it's good to see you. You must be cutting out early tonight, huh?"

Jerold nodded.

"Yeah, I guess so."

Neither of them spoke again as they rode the elevator to the basement level.

"See you tomorrow, buddy," Marc called out as he walked quickly to the security desk.

Jerold took his time as he approached the desk, where Jason, as usual, was in his place.

"Have a nice night, Mr. Volker," Jason said as he opened the door for him.

"Thanks, Jason," Jerold replied with weariness in his voice.

Jerold was feeling really tired, which was unusual. He could work longer and harder than anyone else, and he prided himself on that. Lunch breaks or time off were interruptions in what mattered. This time, though, he trudged to the car as if he were carrying heavy weights. Tossing his stuff into the back seat, Jerold sat down and turned the keys in the ignition. As the car sprang to life, he eased it out of the garage and into the downtown traffic. He had just pulled out onto the highway toward

Darcy's condo when his cell phone buzzed, making him jump and nearly lose control of the vehicle. He pulled the phone out of his pocket and looked. It was a call. Darcy. He pushed the answer button.

"You scared me to death!" he called out into the phone.

"Well, hello to you, too," she replied. She quickly calmed, though, and continued, "I'm sorry. I should have thought. I just wanted to make sure you were coming. I didn't want you to blow me off tonight."

Jerold took a deep breath and answered, "Yeah, I'm coming. I'm just getting on 75 now. I should be there in a few minutes."

"Good," she replied. "Okay. I'll see you then. I love you. Good-bye."

"Good-bye," Jerold replied as he snapped the phone shut.

He chided himself again for being such a baby. He had almost convinced himself that he was acting like a nut when his cell phone buzzed again. Instinctively he thought of Darcy and how she could pester him. He grabbed the phone and prepared to answer. It wasn't a call, though. A text message was being sent. That unnerved him and, as soon as he could, he pulled off of the highway into the parking lot at a roadside restaurant. He eased the BMW to a stop under a lonely tree next to the lot, took the phone and pushed the button to receive the text.

Help me. Come home.

Jerold was not really upset by the latest message. Actually, he was becoming numb to them. He stared at the phone for a few minutes. Once again, there was no identification and no number. He knew where it came from, though. The question of where had been answered. The issue was who and, maybe even more importantly, why. In the shade of the lonely tree, Jerold took a few minutes to think, and in the quietness of that moment, he decided what to do.

He backed the car out of the parking space and sped back onto the highway, driving almost mechanically to Darcy's condo, where he parked the BMW in his usual spot in the front and slowly got out. He walked to Darcy's door and knocked. She opened it right away.

"There you are. I was beginning to worry."

Jerold didn't say anything, which was odd.

Darcy continued, "What's the matter? Are you all right?"

Jerold handed her the phone and sat down on the couch in her living room. Darcy took the phone and read the latest message. She frowned. Neither of them spoke for a few awkward minutes.

Darcy broke the silence. "Well, when are we going?"

It was Jerold's turn to be puzzled this time.

"What do you mean, 'when are we going?' We're not going anywhere."

Darcy shook her head.

"You know exactly what I'm talking about. You've got to go and you know it. I'm going with you."

Jerold tried to interrupt, "Wait, you're not – I'm not –"

Darcy wouldn't hear any of it.

"This is going to eat you alive until you find out what's

happening. I know you. You won't be able to do anything until you find out what's going on. I'm definitely going, too. I won't let you go by yourself."

Jerold sat on the couch in silence. Darcy didn't often get aggressive. When she did, it was best just to go along and not challenge her. Besides, she was right. He knew it. He would not rest until he found out who or what this was.

"When do you think we can go?" she asked as she sat next to him on the couch. "I've got some sick days at school that I can use."

"I think I'd like to go right away," Jerold finally said. "I'll call Lonaker tonight. Patrisse will cover for me for a few days. I'm sure that if we leave tomorrow, we can settle this before the weekend."

"Good," Darcy replied, "I'll call in now. I can pack a few things and we can leave first thing in the morning."

While Darcy went to call her school and pack a few things, Jerold sat on the couch and watched reruns of *The Andy Griffith Show*. Lots of laughs were coming from the television. It was an episode in which Aunt Bea and other ladies in Mayberry were caught up in some gossip about Andy. It was a funny episode, but Jerold didn't see much of it. His mind was not in Mayberry…

Pikesville was the typical small town where everyone knew everyone and there were no secrets. Jerold remembered how the ladies in Miller's Drug Store would gather on the pretense of looking at the latest magazines. What they really did was share the latest gossip. Jerold heard about whose marriage was in trouble and who was seen in the pub in the wee hours of the morning. Nothing that happened in Pikesville escaped the magazine rack gossip hounds. He hated their gossip and wanted to tell them that. If he could have mustered the nerve, he would have let them know that it wasn't any of their business what others did or didn't do. A lot of things he wished to say never got said...

"Hey, do you want to eat?" Darcy broke into Jerold's thoughts.

"Oh yeah, uh, I guess so," Jerold stammered. "Do you have anything here, Darce? I'd rather not go out tonight."

"Sure," she replied, "If you can take my cooking!"

Darcy smiled and went to the kitchen. She made some spaghetti and in a few minutes they were sitting around her kitchen table.

"How do you like it?" she asked.

"Oh this," he replied, nodding to the spaghetti. "I like it just fine. You're a good cook, Darce."

"Yeah, right," she retorted as she finished eating. "So, what time will you be here tomorrow?"

Jerold spoke between bites.

"I'll get here early. It's about three hours or so to Pikesville. I think we should get there first thing in the morning, so be ready to leave a little before six."

At home, throwing a few things into an overnight bag completed Jerold's packing. Mr. Lonaker had a few questions when Jerold called him, but he let him go because he had accumulated quite a few sick days. Patrisse was a bit more inquisitive, however. Jerold explained to her the third message, and he could tell she was bothered. She relaxed a little when he told her that he and Darcy were going to Pikesville. She promised to manage things for the day and added that she and Darrion were praying, but that didn't seem to comfort him. He went to bed before ten. Sleep was elusive and when it finally came, Jerold's dreams were of a little drug store in Pikesville.

His alarm went off at four forty-five, but Jerold was already up and showered. What this day would hold, he didn't know, but he was ready. It was different putting on jeans and a "Duke" t-shirt to start the day; it had been a long time since he had dressed so casually. Jerold went into the kitchen and thought about eating, but he rarely kept anything in there. It was a kitchen for show more than use. He did find some orange juice, poured it into a clean glass and sat at the table to drink it. Going back to Pikesville was not something he had thought he would ever do, but something was pulling him there. Of that, he was certain.

He threw his bag into the back of the BMW. It was still dark in Cincinnati as he headed out, and the street lights illuminated the nearly abandoned highway. It would be an hour or so before most of the Queen City woke up to a new day, and by then, Jerold and Darcy would be in Kentucky. Jerold had barely stepped out of the car at Darcy's condo when she came out of the front door, wearing khaki shorts and a Bengals' sweatshirt, her blonde hair pulled back in a ponytail. He had not seen her as casual as this in a while, and he noticed, once again, how pretty she was. He trotted up to meet her and grab her bag.

"Good morning," she called out to him. "You're early."

Settling Darcy and her bag, Jerold said, "Hey, why don't you try to sleep? I can drive for a while."

"You don't mind?" Darcy asked, yawning. "You'll be okay, won't you?"

"Sure, I'll be fine."

Darcy adjusted her seat and leaned back. In just a few minutes, Jerold was glad to hear her quiet, steady breathing. He wanted some time to think as much as he wanted her to rest. As he crossed from Ohio into Kentucky, the sky was turning different shades of pink and purple. With the coming sunrise, Jerold could see houses with just a few lights on, indicating that people were getting up and getting ready for the day. He remembered early mornings back home...

The address was 203 Cambridge. It wasn't anything special, but to Jerold and Janice it was home. Jerold must've been no older than three or four. Janice, his sister, was two years older, and she never let him forget that. Jerold had not recalled these memories for quite a while, but they were surprisingly fresh. He remembered his little bedroom, just off of the living room. His room was small, but very much a boy's room. His bedspread, sheets and curtains all displayed the logos of every Major League baseball team. He had seen them once in the Sears catalog and begged and begged until his mom gave in. Mom. Jerold remembered her, too. She would come in every morning and gently nudge Jerold awake. She always called out to him, "Come on lazy bones. It's time to get up. The day won't wait for you."

"Lazy bones." Jerold chuckled audibly. It had been such a long time since he'd heard that. It sounded so innocent and simple. *Lazy bones,* he thought; *not any-more, Mom.*

Mom always made breakfast, too. Jerold, Janice and their dad never left home without having something for breakfast. It wasn't too fancy, but every day began with pancakes, French toast or cereal.

Jerold had not thought of his mother for a long time. Now, though, he couldn't get her out of his mind.

Mom was also there when things didn't go so well. There was the time that Jerold, no older than four, fell from the stone wall that encased the driveway. They had just finished breakfast and he had followed Janice and Dad. Dad was going to drop Janice off at school. Jerold had hopped up on the wall that lined the driveway and waved to them as they pulled off. Once they turned off of Cambridge Street, he pretended that he was in the circus, walking the high wire. Of course, he fell. He scraped his knee and it bled a little. Jerold ran crying into the house. His mom picked him up and set him on her lap. She dabbed his knee with a washcloth and put a bandage on it.

As Jerold thought about it now, it didn't seem like much. It was a nice feeling, though. The dark was almost gone, and the sky was beginning to brighten. Jerold was alone with his thoughts...

Jerold had an embarrassing problem, especially for boys. He was afraid of the dark. Sleeping at night in a dark bedroom terrified him. Janice just made fun of him. What would you expect from an older sister? His dad didn't understand and would try to show him there was nothing to fear. He told him to be a man and be strong. Jerold tried, but the fear was pretty strong, too. He recalled one night in particular. He'd been crying, as usual. Maybe the room was darker than usual. After trying to reason with him for quite a while, his dad scolded him and left him alone in his dark room. Jerold was in bed, sniffling, when his mom came in quietly. She knelt beside his bed and whispered to him. "Jerold, I have something for you."

She was carrying an old paper sack from which she pulled out an old, brown teddy bear.

"Here, Jerold. I want you to have this. It was mine. He used to help me not be afraid, and I think he'll help you."

Jerold clutched the bear tightly to his chest. His mom patted his head and kissed him on the cheek.

"Now, good night, dear, sleep well."

There had been tears on Jerold's four-year-old face then and there were tears on the older Jerold's face, now. Darcy noticed.

"Hey, are you okay," she asked.

Jerold was startled that she was awake and had somewhat invaded his thoughts.

"Uh, yeah, I'm fine."

"But weren't you crying?"

"Forget it. Let's stop to eat. I'm hungry."

Chapter Four

*T*hey stopped at a restaurant somewhere near Louisville, where they said little as they ate breakfast and lingered awhile in the gift shop. In less than an hour, they were back on the road. Darcy was wide awake and ready to talk.

"Before we stopped to eat, you were upset. Did anything happen while I was asleep? You didn't get another message or something, did you?"

Jerold shook his head as he eased the car back on the highway.

"No. No messages," he answered.

"Well, what was it that had you so upset? I know something isn't right."

Jerold interrupted, "Darce, I don't want to talk about it!"

Darcy wouldn't be intimidated, though.

"Come on, Jerold. I'm taking days off work to go back to the small town you grew up in and have never mentioned until now. You've never said a word about your childhood to me. Now you get these weird messages. I have no idea what's going on, and maybe you don't either, but we're in this together."

When she said this, Jerold looked briefly into her face. She was sincere and practically begging to help him.

"Come on, Jerold. What's going on? Tell me something."

Jerold swallowed hard. He wasn't sure he wanted to tell Darcy anything. He knew, though, that her tenacious personality wouldn't let him have a moment of rest unless he told her something. He also knew that she cared. Really, above anything else, she truly cared. She had jumped into this without knowing any more than he did. Actually, she knew even less than he knew. He owed her.

He swallowed deeply and said, "This isn't a pretty story and I don't know what we'll find in Pikesville this morning, but I know what was there when I left. When today ends, I don't know what you'll think, but you're right. You deserve to know something."

He paused for a moment and she turned to face him. He stared at the highway.

"Darcy, I haven't told you-- or anyone, for that matter-- much about my family. I'm not sure how much I can tell you now, but I'll try to talk some. You already know that I have a sister, Janice. She's a couple of years older than I am. I was born in Pikesville, but Janice was born in Louisville. Before I was born, my dad worked in management for a big manufacturer in Louisville. He was working hard, making money, and things were looking great. He was moving up the ladder. At least, that's what I was told. When Mom was carrying me, something happened at the company where Dad worked. They called it an 'economic slowdown.' The bottom line was that, because he didn't have the education some others had, he was part of the necessary cutbacks. He lost his job.

Our family moved to Pikesville because Dad knew someone who had a little bank there. So, Dad went to work in the bank at Pikesville. He went from overseeing and participating in million dollar deals around the world to counting nickels and dimes for dirt farmers. I suppose that could make anyone bitter. It makes me bitter just thinking about it. By the time I came along, my dad's dreams were gone and he just went to work. He pushed us to succeed, though, Janice and me. I suppose he especially pushed me because I was his son. I needed to get the education and have the necessary tools so that no one would ever be able to say, 'We don't need you.' To settle for less than I could have would be tragic. Ambition and striving for excellence were instilled in me when I was young because my dad believed you had to be tough for the challenges of the mean, cruel world. That's how it was in our family. That's where I learned to be the man I am today."

"Did you and your dad have any, you know, fun?" Darcy asked.

"Of course, Dad was fun sometimes. He was always there for the big moments of my life in Pikesville. He was at every football game. Friday night football was always big. Dad would spend the whole day at the bank talking to anyone who would listen about how the Pirates would win big over that week's opponent. By the time the game rolled around, he was more charged up than I was. When we won, which was a lot, we'd celebrate. The team would go to the Dari Ring and meet the cheerleaders and the rest of the kids. Dad would go home and prepare our own 'victory party.' Then when I got back we'd celebrate. Dad would get some sodas and make burritos. I'm not sure why he made burritos all of the time, but – I guess that's all he knew how to make. Then we'd sit at the kitchen table and go over the game. When we won the state championship, he could hardly stand it. Those were some of the best times of my life."

There was an awkward pause as they continued to drive the highway. The bright rays of the sun peeked through gathering clouds. It looked like a storm might be on the way. Darcy just waited. As they passed an old convenience store, Jerold spoke again.

"I remember when I graduated. He was excited for me and gave me a hundred dollars. That was a lot back then. 'Make good and don't hang around here,' I remember him saying. I think he might have been kidding a little, but I took him at his word. I never went back."

Darcy furrowed her brow.

"Why, Jerold?"

"I don't know, Darce. I'm tired of talking about it, though. Get that new CD I bought last week, and let's hear some music for a while."

♪ ♪ ♪

They were less than fifty miles from Pikesville as the sweet, melodic sounds of jazz filled the BMW. Darcy was content listening to the music. She didn't know the

39

highway or how close they were to Pikesville. In her mind, though, she thought about how close she was to Jerold. He would never admit it, ever. That was certain. But over the last several months, Darcy had grown to love him. Her friends warned her that he might not ever return that love. They told her that she was investing in a relationship that could bear no returns. But Darcy had always been head-strong. She invested herself anyway. She couldn't help it. Now she looked at him as he drove and smiled. There was something in there worth loving. She knew it.

♪ ♪ ♪

As the low bass notes of the jazz quartet filled the car, Jerold thought about the situation in which he now found himself. This was clearly the most impulsive and irrational thing he had ever done, leaving the comfort and security of his big office for this foolish road trip to a place he had sworn he would never visit again. Not only was he on this fool's errand, but he had told Darcy about his family. He had to be crazy to allow her to come with him. He didn't know what exactly he would find there, but he knew there was no way it could be good. How could he allow Darcy to have anything to do with, well, his past? She used the word "love" a lot, but Jerold wouldn't go there. He couldn't. He did like her, though, and wanted to keep seeing her. All of that was in jeopardy now. When she found out where he came from and what had happened, it would be over. How could he have been so dumb? He sighed and looked over at her as she smiled. Jerold breathed deeply and gripped the wheel even more tightly. Soon, they would arrive. He would see how long she smiled then.

The BMW sped down the Kentucky highway. Jerold noticed the fields and the occasional farms that dotted the countryside, and he knew their destination was not too far up the road. His apprehension of what was coming was abruptly sidetracked by another memory. He saw it in the distance before they passed by it: the Roadway Diner, a fixture in this part of the country, standing as an ancient sentinel to greet those coming into the Tri-County area...

The Roadway Diner was a cinder block building. When Jerold was a kid, the building had been painted white with blue trim. Looking at it now as he passed, he saw that it was still white, though the paint was peeling in places. The trim, however, was an odd shade of green. The sign out front was different, but the name was the same: "Roadway Diner." Jerold's mind went back to when he was a little boy. He had to have been about six years old which would have made Janice about eight. They did not get to eat out a lot. It had to be a special occasion, so they were thrilled when they got home from school and mom told them to stay clean because they were going out to eat. They didn't know why, but they knew that something special was happening. Janice and Jerold did their best to not get too dirty playing. Dad came home from the bank early, and that was odd, too. He never came home early.

Mom had them all pile into the family car. He and Janice could tell that they had been talking and that it had been serious, but that's what parents did. He and Janice didn't care. They were going out to eat. Jerold talked about having apple pie after dinner and was hinting about it pretty loudly. Janice reminded him that he would have to eat all of his dinner first. That brought about another argument between them. Mom tried to hush them, but it was Dad who threatened them with a whipping if they didn't quiet down. That restored order. Jerold didn't say anything else about apple pie, but he sure did think about it. They got to the Roadway Diner and Dad parked the car. Inside, they found a booth for the four of them away from the rest of the weeknight crowd. Dad asked what they wanted to eat and ordered it. Jerold was surprised when he mentioned to the waiter that they would all want pie afterward and that his boy wanted apple.

While they ate, they laughed and talked about a lot of things. They even discussed going on a family vacation real soon. They might go to the big amusement park in Ohio! Jerold could only imagine how much fun that might be. Then, things changed. Mom started talking about going to the doctor. She had not been feeling well. Mom and Dad weren't laughing anymore. Dad mentioned something about some kind of therapy, which Jerold didn't understand at the time. Mom said "cancer," but Jerold didn't know what that was. He asked Janice about it later that night, but she didn't want to talk. Jerold remembered that his apple pie hadn't been nearly as good as he had thought it would be…

Darcy didn't ask any more questions as they neared Pikesville and Jerold was glad. He had talked more than he wanted already. The sign ahead said, "Welcome to Pikesville." Below that, in smaller letters, it said,

"Population 645." It was freshly painted, so Jerold knew that town still existed. Darcy noticed it, too, and sat up in the passenger seat. She turned down the music and looked at Jerold.

"Well, we're here. What do we do now?"

It was a good question, and one to which Jerold hadn't really given much thought.

"I guess we need to go downtown," he finally answered. "We'll see what downtown looks like and if there's anyone or anything there that I might recognize."

That seemed like a reasonable plan, good enough for Darcy. They drove through the farmlands surrounding the little town of Pikesville, and Darcy saw more cattle and hay than she had ever seen before. Every now and then, a silo or a barn would break up the wide open fields. Then they rounded a bend in the road and the farmland ceased. As they entered Pikesville, the highway became Main Street so there wasn't any need to find an exit or an access ramp. Darcy took it all in. Being from Columbus, she had not seen much of small town America. Jerold, though, knew the place well. It seemed to have not changed in the twenty years or so he had been gone. There was the gas station on the corner. There was the Feed and Seed on Main. Right next to it was the bank, and next to the bank was Miller's Drug Store. Mr. Miller had died before Jerold graduated, and his daughter, Martha, had taken over. She wasn't married then and Jerold imagined that hadn't changed. Jerold figured she still ran the place. He parked the BMW in one of the parking spaces in front of the Feed and Seed.

"Let's go to Miller's and see if Martha is still there. I'm sure someone will know her, at least."

They walked down the brick sidewalk as the few people out on Main Street on Wednesday morning got a special treat. It was rare that a BMW was spotted in this town. At the door of the drug store, they paused to look at all the hand bills taped randomly to the window. One or two advertised lost dogs. There was one for a hay ride at the Methodist church, and another for a chili supper at the VFW. There was even one announcing a professional wrestling bout in nearby Eddyville. Jerold smiled. A long time ago, he had been responsible for hanging those and keeping them current. He felt for the poor kid whose job it now was to keep the flyers updated.

They walked through the door and back in time. Miller's Drug Store was not much different than it had been twenty years ago. Even then, it had not been much different than it was when Mr. Miller opened it. There was still a magazine rack in the corner. Jerold saw it and glanced away quickly. There were still shelves of over-the-counter pills and tablets in the back and an assortment of unusual, but necessary things on the shelves in the middle. Modernization had come, though, in the form of a new cash register. A scanner replaced the push-button register Jerold had used. There were a few customers in the drug store; a couple of ladies examining the various pills for arthritis, a young mother looking at medicine for teething babies, and an older gentleman talking with a lady behind the counter. Though her hair was graying ever so slightly, Jerold recognized her. It was Martha. When the older man had the information he needed, he thanked Martha and left. Jerold and Darcy approached the counter. Martha stared for just a moment, her mind drifting back to a face she knew she recognized.

"Oh my heavens," she exclaimed, "Is that you, Jerold Volker? It is! Oh my goodness, I can't believe it!"

She ran out from behind the counter, startling the little old ladies who were discussing arthritis pills.

Jerold stood still while Martha embraced him in a hug.

"It's been so long, honey! What have you been up to and what brings you back here?"

She then noticed Darcy and backed away a step.

"Is this the wife?" she asked as she turned toward Darcy.

Jerold shook his head.

"Martha, it's good to see you. This is Darcy Coulton, a friend of mine."

Darcy turned toward Jerold and rolled her eyes at his introduction of her as a "friend." She politely took Martha's hand, though, and smiled.

"It's nice to meet you, Martha."

"Well come over to the table here and sit down."

They walked through the cluttered store to the back, where two tables served as a place to drink sodas, and they sat down, Darcy next to Jerold and Martha across from him.

"Tell me, what brings you all the way back to Pikesville? I heard you made it big in Cleveland after you left Duke."

"Cincinnati," Jerold corrected.

Jerold paused. He had not seen Martha for over twenty years. How do you explain some weird text messages to someone you haven't talked to in a two decades?

"I just wanted to poke around the old place," Jerold finally replied. "You know, catch up on what's going on."

Martha took the cue very well. It seemed she was an expert on all that was going on in Pikesville. She told them about all the scandals that had happened since Jerold left. She mentioned several folks, many of whom Jerold did not know, who had left and gone on to other things, and she talked about how the school was still standing, but the sports teams had been forced to merge with Eddyville about ten miles down the road. The Pikesville Pirates were no more. Jerold was saddened by that, but didn't interrupt. He let Martha continue for about five minutes. Darcy was hanging on every word, looking and hoping for a clue. At last, Martha paused for a breath. Jerold seized the opportunity.

"Martha," he jumped in, "do you remember my family's old house on Cambridge Street? My sister Janice and I grew up there. Is it still around?"

Martha looked down and breathed in deeply.

"Yes, the house is still there, mostly."

Jerold was puzzled by that.

"Mostly? What do you mean?"

It was clear to Martha that Jerold did not know.

"It happened after you left. There was a fire. It was awful; the whole volunteer fire department came out. The house was really messed up. It's still standing, though; the county hasn't torn it down."

Darcy was listening closely and Jerold was suddenly

intent, too.

"What about my dad, Martha; what happened to him? Is he around town somewhere?"

Martha looked down. Though she liked to talk, she suddenly seemed not to like this conversation.

"He died in the fire, Jerold," she finally told him, her voice strained with emotion. "I'm sorry; I didn't know you didn't know. I mean, I knew you weren't at the funeral, but-- I'm sorry, Jerold. I really am."

Jerold was shocked by the news.

"When?" he asked. "When did this happen?"

"I guess it was about ten years ago or so."

After a few moments of awkward silence, Martha excused herself to check on customers. They promised to get together again before Jerold left town. As Jerold and Darcy walked slowly back to the car, Darcy didn't know what to say. Stunned, Jerold said nothing. The house where he had lived had burned down, his father had died and he didn't even know. He was pretty sure Janice knew, but they never talked. That was his doing. She had tried to reach him many times, but he had refused to be reached. He could only imagine what Darcy must be thinking. It was too late to hide anything at this point.

"I want to see it," Jerold finally announced as he and Darcy walked to the car.

"See what?"

"My old house," Jerold told her.

Darcy might not have been sure this was a good idea, but what could she have said? They were in Pikesville and had to do something. Without talking, they drove down Main Street and found Cambridge. Sure enough, at the end of Cambridge was a burned, dilapidated house, with two crumbling stone walls around the driveway. It looked like it had been abandoned, which was true. Things didn't move very fast in Pikesville and no one was pushing to do anything, so the town had not leveled it. It remained a crumbling, charred reminder of what had once been a home. Jerold stopped the BMW at the edge of the driveway, and stared at what was left of the old house. Darcy silently took it all in. The address was still on the mailbox: 203 Cambridge Street. At last, Jerold Volker had come home.

Chapter Five

*T*hey stared at the burned-out house for a few minutes before Darcy spoke.

"Well, what do you want to do now? Should we go in?"

Jerold shook his head.

"No, not we. I'm going to take you back to town. If you're okay with it, I'll leave you at the courthouse to check the records and see what you can find out about my dad and when he died. There should be a death certificate. Maybe there will be a few newspaper records, too. I don't know. Just see what you can find, will you? There are a lot of questions and things I just don't know."

Darcy was hesitant at first, but she agreed and Jerold drove her back down Main Street. In just a few minutes they were in front of the courthouse.

"I'll drop you off here and pick you up in an hour or so."

"Don't worry about me," she replied. "Are you sure you're okay? You're going back to the house, aren't you?"

"Yeah, Darce, I am. I don't know. It's just a burned-up, falling down old house, but for some reason, I need to go there. Who knows what I'll find when I get there? I just know that I have to see it."

"Be careful," Darcy told him as she stood by the driver's side window. "I love you."

"Thanks," Jerold replied. "See you in a little while."

Jerold watched Darcy walk up the steps of the old courthouse, carrying a notebook she had brought, just in case it was needed. He saw her open the heavy door and slip away inside.

Now Jerold was alone on his quest for answers. He pulled the BMW back onto Main Street, and for a fleeting moment was tempted to just keep on driving down Main until it turned into the highway again. Just keep on driving and not look back. It had happened once before...

On the morning after his high school graduation, Jerold and his father were eating breakfast. From the kitchen window they noticed how the sun shone brightly against a blue sky. Summer would arrive soon. They were discussing Jerold's plans for the future, a discussion Jerold dreaded. Plans had been made a long time ago for Jerold to leave Pikesville. After graduation he would go to Louisville, where a summer job was waiting for him, thanks to one of Dad's friends, who had some connections. It was a good opportunity to save money and get some experience before enrolling at the University of Louisville in the fall. That plan had been made for months, long before Jerold had started dating Kathy.

Kathy was unlike any other girl Jerold had ever met in high school. She wasn't a cheerleader, or even a football fan. She wasn't interested in Jerold because he was a popular jock. She liked him because of who he was. They talked about dreams and hopes for the future. They talked about books that they liked to read and movies that they wanted to see. She made Jerold laugh. Jerold had seen her at prom just a few weeks from graduation and had been interested. He had spoken to her the following week and they had started dating. A time of reckoning was coming, and Jerold knew it. He was right.

They sat at the kitchen table eating pancakes. His dad was happy, eager for his son's future.

"It was a nice ceremony, Jerold, and I'm proud of you. You've earned a ton of scholarship money, and you did a good job on your speech. Everyone said so. Now, how is the packing coming along? George said he would be ready for you sometime this week."

"Dad," Jerold said timidly, "uh, I wanted to talk to you about that."

"Okay," his dad answered, "shoot."

"Well, I know we've had these plans for a long time, but I was kind of hoping that maybe I could stay here this summer and work at Miller's."

His father erupted. "No way! Are you crazy! This is the chance of a lifetime. You can't throw this away. What's the matter with you, boy?! You're not afraid or nervous, are you?"

"No, it's not that, it's just that Kathy and I thought I could stay."

"A girl," his dad exclaimed. "You can't be serious!

You can't give up this chance to spend the summer chasing some silly girl. No, Jerold. I won't allow you to be stupid…"

The argument carried on for several more minutes, as Jerold recalled it. His dad was not moved and, in the end, Jerold relented. He did have a future ahead of him. Maybe he could make Kathy understand. His bags had been packed and later that afternoon he threw them into his car. He drove to Kathy's house intending to do the impossible. They could stay close, he argued. Louisville wasn't that far. Making a lot of money was good, and he promised he would not forget her.

His best effort on the table, Jerold hoped with all that was in him that she might understand. She didn't. She cried and asked him to leave. Anger began building in Jerold as he stormed from her house and drove home. The next morning Jerold left Pikesville. Louisville was the beginning of his successful climb. He tried to become what his father had challenged him to be and he never came back to Pikesville--until now.

§ § §

Darcy went to the directory on the wall of the courthouse. She wasn't sure what she should be looking for, so she scanned the names and numbers on the sign, finally settling on an office called "County Records" on the second floor. She walked down the big hallway and climbed the marble steps to the second floor, where an arrow on the wall by the stairs pointed out where the offices were. The arrow led her down the hall. Gold letters on the window of the door said, "County Records."

Under the title was a name: Eleanor Woods. Darcy would begin with her.

ſ ſ ſ

Jerold's mind was still back a few years when a car pulled up behind him at the stop sign. The blaring of its horn brought him back to the present. Jerold didn't drive straight onto the highway and away from Pikesville. Instead, he turned back to Cambridge Street. As Jerold pulled up, once again, in front of the driveway with the crumbling stone walls around it, he got out of the car and walked slowly up the drive before coming to the front door of the house. The screen door wasn't there anymore, so he put his hand directly on the door handle and turned. He wasn't sure what he expected to see when he went in, but he knew it was time.

Right away the damage the fire had caused hit Jerold hard. The walls were blackened and some of the beams supporting the roof were exposed. There were pieces of carpet and a lot of exposed wood floors, and water had ruined the few things still standing. It was a mess. In spite of how damaged it was, though, Jerold recognized this house. For about eighteen years, this had been his home. In what had been the kitchen, a few chairs were tossed about and a refrigerator stood against a wall that was still standing. Jerold took it all in for a few minutes and then walked through what had once been the living room. The fire had been bad here, and there wasn't much left. Jerold noticed beer cans and cigarette butts, evidence that looters or petty thieves had visited before he had. The hallway that led to the bedrooms caught his eye. As Jerold looked down the hall, something in him gave way. This was the place where his dad had died. There were so many emotions swirling within him. Questions filled his mind with anger and frustration: *Why? What happened? What happened to us? This is your fault. You did this!*

Jerold looked down the hallway at the first bedroom, Janice's. He didn't want to, but he began thinking about the last time he had seen Janice in this house...

Jerold was a sophomore and already a football star. He was cocky, probably too much so, and, like a lot of high school kids, only concerned about himself. Janice was graduating from high school and Dad was thrilled. Plans for Janice's future had been Dad's main concern for months. Throughout her senior year, he told her how she could get into either Louisville or Kentucky. She had great grades and qualified for all kinds of scholarships, and he had saved money, too, for her to go to college. This was his plan, and a good one, but it wasn't Janice's plan. She fought with him for the last three months of her high school career. She was an excellent student and could do anything, but what she wanted to do was go to the community college about an hour away, study to be a nurse and continue her relationship with Tony, who had graduated a year earlier. They fought hard and long and there were many tears. After she graduated, the ultimatum came: "You either go to college or you can leave." Jerold remembered that fight well. Dad had stood at the end of the hallway, right where Jerold now stood, while Janice was in her room, crying and noisily gathering her things. She had burst from her room and screamed, "I'm leaving!" as she ran out the front door. Jerold saw his dad angrily try to follow her and bring her back. Jerold was in bed already when he came back, alone. Though he did not fully understand it at the time, he knew he was now his dad's last hope...

Jerold stood at the end of the hallway. *I didn't understand, Janice. Why? Why didn't you ever come back? Why didn't you call?*

His anger also flared toward his father. *Dad, how could you let her go? Why did you have to make that stupid 'my way or else' remark? You knew what she would do! If you hadn't done that, she would have been here, for you, for us. You wouldn't have died alone.*

The anger brought fresh tears to Jerold's eyes and for the second time that day, he cried. Jerold paused at the bathroom. The sink was dirty and the mirror blackened by smoke. He saw the toilet next to the bathtub...

He was in the second grade. On an unusually warm fall day, Jerold ran home from school by himself. Janice was on a field trip to the museum in Louisville, and wouldn't get back until later that night. Dad was still at work at the bank. Jerold looked forward to spending time with his mom, just the two of them. No doubt she would have a snack ready for him. Then they would play. Maybe they would play catch in the backyard. They might build something next to the garage, a birdhouse or a scarecrow for her garden. Perhaps they would play a game inside. It didn't matter, really. Jerold sprinted to the edge of the driveway, ran along the top of the rock wall to the porch. He threw open the door and rushed into the house, yelling, "Mom! Mom, I'm home!"

There was no answer. That was unusual. He ran to the kitchen, where she must be hiding, waiting to surprise him. He jumped around the corner, expecting to see her crouching there and laughing. There was no one.

"Mom," he called out, "where are you?"

Jerold thought maybe she was out in the backyard already. He looked out the kitchen window and saw the garden and the tomato plants swaying gently in the wind. The tire swing moved just a little in the breeze. Nobody was out there, though.

Taking a nap was possible. It wasn't like her to do that, but maybe. He walked down the hallway toward her room. That was when he passed the bathroom and when he saw her. She was kneeling in front of the toilet. He had become used to her without hair, but he had never seen her so sick. She looked up and he saw her sad, tired eyes, filled with pain. Even to a seven-year-old, it seemed she would give the world to not have her son see her like this. She threw up again, violently. Jerold ran to her and put his arms around her. She held him and tried to get to her feet.

That was the last night his mom had spent at 203 Cambridge Street. She had gone to the hospital the next day. Jerold paused at the fire-ravaged bathroom. He saw the toilet still there. Tears flowing down his cheeks, he turned away from the bathroom. His eye fell upon the door to the little bedroom at the end of the hall. His bedroom. For some reason, the door was closed. Taking a few steps down the hall, he reached for the door knob...

Jerold had been to the hospital a few times to see his mother. Dad had told both him and Janice it was important that they go. Their mom needed to see them. Jerold went and tried his best to make his mom smile. He drew pictures for her and made her cards. His classmates spent a whole art class making pictures for him to take to her. One night, after an especially hard day for her, he sneaked his teddy bear into the hospital. He didn't want his dad to see. When his dad and Janice had gone to the cafeteria, Jerold offered the teddy bear to his mom.

"Here, Mom, he'll help you feel better. You won't be afraid."

His mother smiled from her hospital bed.

"No, Jerold, you keep Teddy. You're going to need him and he'll need you, too. I'll be all right."

Jerold didn't understand what she meant by all right, but he found out the next day. He and Janice got home from school and right away they knew something was different, wrong. Dad's car was in the drive, and so was Mrs. Walters' car, the visiting nurse. They ran into the house.

"What's going on?" Jerold remembered Janice asking.

"Kids," Mrs. Walters said, "your daddy needs to talk to you."

Jerold remembered that conversation well. He had never seen tears in his dad's eyes until that time. There were only a few, but they were there. Mom was really sick and God thought she shouldn't hurt anymore, he tried to say. Mom died, and she wouldn't be coming home. Janice had a few questions and Jerold supposed that Dad answered them. All he could remember was the numb feeling that someone who really loved him was gone and wasn't coming back.

The next few days went by really fast. There was a church service called a funeral. Jerold watched as people came by and cried over his mom's body in the casket. Dad told him Mom wasn't really there, and Jerold did his best to understand that. They went to the cemetery beside the church and he watched as they put the casket into the ground. For Jerold, there were no tears at the funeral service. It was all too different and strange. His sister cried, though. They went back to the house later that day, and a lot of people came by to visit. Jerold just hung out in the backyard, away from everyone. He didn't know what to feel or what to say.

As the day went on, people went home and Dad called him in for supper. The three of them ate burritos and had sodas. None of them said very much. After supper, Dad told them to get ready for bed, then, they could watch television for a while as he cleaned up the kitchen. Janice and Jerold put on their pajamas. Jerold had on his new baseball ones, with all the teams' logos on them. They watched television for about an hour or so and then Dad announced it was time for bed. Jerold went to his little bedroom and pulled down the covers. In a few minutes, his dad came and tucked him in, turned out the lights and closed the door. The room got dark, very dark. At that moment it all hit Jerold. His mom was gone. She was dead. He wouldn't see her again. He began to sob hard, holding Teddy tightly to his chest as he wept. His dad came in as soon as he heard Jerold's sobs. He clicked on the light and saw his little boy curled up in bed clutching a ragged teddy bear.

"Jerold, what are you doing? What's the matter, boy?"

Jerold couldn't say anything.

His dad reached down to him.

"Jerold, you can't cry like this and be a big baby. You know your mom wouldn't want that. Now, be a big boy and stop your crying."

Dad sat down next to him on the bed.

"Jerold, I know this is going to be hard, but you've got to be tough. You and I can't go around crying. It will upset your sister. You've got to be strong, son."

Jerold sat up in bed, still holding the teddy. Dad noticed the teddy and shook his head.

"Jerold, you're a big boy now. You can't go around dragging a teddy bear. You've got to act your age. You're not a baby."

Dad took the teddy, or maybe Jerold gave it to him. He didn't remember, and it didn't matter. What did matter, though, was that he never cried again for his mother. He was strong. He wasn't a baby...

Right now, though, Jerold did feel small and sad.

"Dad, why did this have to happen?" he said aloud, his anger rising. "Why did Momma have to leave? I'm tired of being tough and strong! I wanted to cry, Dad. I wanted to be upset. Why did I have to be so tough? Why were you? Why did you drive me and Janice away? Why did you take Teddy? I needed him! I hate... I hate..!"

"What is it you hate, Jerold?" a voice said from behind him.

Jerold was jolted back to reality. He turned and saw a man standing behind him in the hall, wearing blue jeans, a gray t-shirt and a red Louisville ball cap. He had a tool belt around his waist and a smile on his bearded face. Jerold stared at him for a few seconds, trying his best to recall a name.

"Who are you?" Jerold asked, surprised that he had not heard anyone enter behind him. "Do I know you?"

"Oh, I think we've met a time or two. I'm the carpenter sent to fix things up around here," the man replied.

♫ ♫ ♫

Darcy stepped up to the counter in the records office. The office was clean and neat; it was obvious that the person in charge knew what he or she was doing. Darcy cleared her throat.

"May I help you?" an elderly African-American woman said as she turned the corner and faced Darcy at the counter. Darcy could see that she walked with a cane.

"Uh, yes, ma'am," Darcy replied. "I would like to get some information, please."

"Okay, honey," the woman said, "I'm Mrs. Woods. Now just who are you and what kind of information are you looking for?"

Darcy cleared her throat.

"I'm Darcy Coulton from Cincinnati and I'm here with a friend of mine. I'm hoping to check out a death certificate or something. My friend's name is Volker. Do you know anyone by that name?"

When she said this, Mrs. Woods raised her eyebrows.

"Volker? Why, you don't mean Joe Volker, do you?"

"Maybe," Darcy answered. "What can you tell me?"

"I've lived here all my life, and I'm pretty sure you mean Joe. Sit right here," Mrs. Woods replied. "I'll be right back."

§ § §

Jerold wasn't sure he had heard this stranger correctly. "Someone sent you to fix things up here?" Jerold asked, wondering who in the world would care about this disaster that was once a house.

"Yep," the fellow replied, "I'm pretty sure this is the place."

The carpenter walked down the hall and came closer to Jerold, who watched him closely. Though this man was a stranger, Jerold didn't feel any fear.

"It's pretty hard to lose someone we love, isn't it? I'm sure you were crushed when your momma died."

Jerold swallowed and then looked the stranger in the eye.

"Wait a minute," he said as he grabbed the carpenter by the shoulder. "How do you know that? How do you know about my mom or me? How do you even know my name?"

"Jerold," the carpenter began, smiling kindly, "I know all about you. I've known about you since before you were born. I also know about your family, and I was here when your mom died."

Jerold struggled to grasp what this stranger was saying. It seemed so unlikely and so ridiculous and yet, he believed it. Somehow, he knew it was true. He studied the man's face and desperately tried to place him. The carpenter continued to smile. He put his hand on Jerold's shoulder and looked into his eyes.

"Jerold, I've been watching you for a long time, too."

Jerold's mind was swirling. The "stranger" had interrupted a very personal moment. Normally this would have enraged and embarrassed Jerold, but it didn't seem to be awkward or intrusive. This carpenter seemed to really know things. Jerold couldn't remember his being around, but it was such a long time ago, and Jerold had chosen to forget many things.

"Do you-- were you," he stammered, "a friend of my dad's?"

The carpenter smiled.

"Yeah," he said, "I guess I was."

Jerold tried to compose himself, but he was intrigued.

"Maybe you can tell me, what happened to him? How did this place get like this?"

The carpenter laughed.

"I'll be glad to help you with that and a lot of other things, too. Why don't we start with the most obvious thing: Jerold, why are you here? What brings you to Pikesville?"

"Okay, I'll tell you. What have I got to lose? I got some anonymous text messages from here. I couldn't figure out who sent them."

The carpenter nodded as he spoke.

"I'm aware of those messages, Jerold."

Jerold was hopeful. Maybe this carpenter was going to reveal something to him.

"So," Jerold began, "did you send them? Why? How am I supposed to help you?"

The carpenter just shook his head.

"No, Jerold, I didn't send them."

"What? I don't get it. If it wasn't you, then who was it?"

Jerold's anger started to show. He was so close to knowing and yet the answer seemed so far away.

"I know who sent them, Jerold," the carpenter said calmly. "I can show you. Do you really want to know?"

Jerold nodded. Things were happening so fast and so strangely that he didn't know what to say.

"Follow me," the carpenter said as he opened the door to Jerold's bedroom.

Jerold stepped in. Through the shadows he saw the charred walls and darkened windows. Old furniture and curtains cluttered the floor. The carpenter went to the light switch on the wall, but Jerold thought he was wasting his time. The electricity had been out since the fire or had been turned off a long time ago. However, when the carpenter flipped the switch, the lights came on in the room. Jerold couldn't believe his eyes. The windows were clean. The walls were painted bright blue. A bedspread with the logos of all the Major League baseball teams was placed neatly on top of the little bed.

Jerold gasped, "What happened? How did you do that?"

The carpenter waved off his questions.

"Jerold," he said pointing to the closet, "the one who texted you is right here."

Jerold couldn't believe what he was seeing or doing. He knew, though, that he had to open that closet. He had to know. Everything seemed to depend upon knowing this truth. He put his hand to the closet door, turned the handle and pulled. It took a second for the light from the room to hit the darkness of the closet. When Jerold looked in he saw a curly-haired little boy, wearing pajamas with baseball logos, and clutching a teddy bear. Jerold was looking at his seven-year-old self.

Chapter Six

Jerold stood silently, just staring at the seven-year-old. The little boy, for his part, simply clutched the teddy bear and continued to look down or away. Jerold noticed that he seemed afraid. Finally, after a minute of awkward silence, he spoke to the carpenter who stood silently beside them.

"I don't understand," he stammered. "This is me? I don't get it. Is this real? Am I dreaming? What's happened here?"

The carpenter smiled again and put his hand on Jerold's shoulder.

"Jerold, there are a lot of things you don't understand."

"I know that," Jerold interrupted, "but this...this is really strange. Tell me, what's going on here? Who is this? Why did he send text messages?"

The carpenter sighed.

"Okay Jerold, you've got a right to know. What is happening to you is real. It is very real, but not in the way you think. You came to the house at 203 Cambridge

Street. It was your home. It is a burned-out, run-down, abandoned house. You walked into the kitchen, the living room, the bathroom and the bedrooms. All of that is real physically. It changed only moments ago. When I came into this room with you, we entered your real home."

Jerold looked at him, puzzled.

"Your real home, Jerold, is your heart. Just like your house on 203 Cambridge is burned out and in ruins, so is your heart. Your house on Cambridge Street is just a picture of your heart, your home."

Jerold stared at the carpenter, trying to grasp what he was hearing.

"So, I'm in some kind of trance or altered state of mind?"

The carpenter laughed.

"No, not some kind of drug-induced consciousness. I have simply pulled back the veil so you get to see the 'real world.' You have a chance to see what is really going on in your life. You've been given a great opportunity."

"This is crazy!" Jerold exclaimed. "I'm getting out of here. This is too strange. I'll go pick up Darcy and we're gone."

"You can go, Jerold," the carpenter replied, "but if you do, then you will miss out on what the text messages were all about and on your chance for change."

Jerold stopped at the end of the hall. A part of him wanted to run, to get far away from Pikesville and this carpenter. Another part of him, though, was clinging with all its might to stay, to get answers. It was that part that won out. Jerold walked back to his old bedroom.

"I'll stay, for a while. So, you're telling me that you are showing me more than just the burned-out, run-down condition of my old house. You are showing me the condition of my heart. That's weird, but I'll go along with it. That doesn't tell me why he is here or how he contacted me."

As Jerold said that, he pointed down to the little boy still cowering in the closet. The carpenter reached out to the boy, and for the first time, the boy seemed to relax. He clutched the bear tightly to his chest as he stood. The carpenter picked him up and held him. The boy put his head on the carpenter's shoulder. The carpenter just held the boy and patted his back. There was a minute or two of silence before he spoke. Jerold just waited.

"Jerold," he finally began, "this is the hardest part. I want you to understand this, because a lot of people don't. If you choose to leave after I tell you this, then I won't try to stop you."

Jerold listened intently.

"When people get hurt in this life they tend to do whatever they can to make sure they don't get hurt again. Some people try to deaden the pain by doing things to numb it and make it go away. Others, when something happens, put up a wall and vow to never step out from behind it. They do it to protect themselves. Unfortunately though, they really put themselves in prison. Many times they don't even know it. They continue through life, maturing and growing in many ways, yet there is a part of them that remains stuck behind the wall. I know that in a lot of people there is a little boy or a little girl who has been hurt and is trying desperately to come out."

Jerold nodded as he took it in.

"When you were seven years old and your mom died, you felt some powerful emotions. You loved her and she loved you. Your love for her was pure. It was given without regard for what might happen. She loved you that way, too. It was and is beautiful, unconditional. She died, though. When she did, you decided you would never love like that again. I know what your dad said. I even know why he said it. You had to be tough. You had to be a man. Because of the pain and the hurt, Jerold, you chose to harden yourself. You wouldn't make yourself vulnerable again. You locked a part of yourself in the closet. I understand what you thought and why you did it. It hurt so much to lose someone you loved that I suppose it made sense to never love again. That boy was safe and would never get hurt. The problem, though, is that in protecting him in that closet, you imprisoned him. He hasn't known the joy of life or loving ever since. He has been desperately trying to reach you. He wants your help. He wants to be free. He wants to love again and live again."

Jerold stood looking at the carpenter and the little boy on his shoulder. He could hardly believe what he was hearing and yet, somehow, he knew it was true.

"I helped him contact you. I can set him free and clean up this place, but you have to let me. You hold the key, Jerold. So, I guess this is the moment. What do you want to do?"

Jerold stood silently, his mind swirling. He had never imagined this would be what he would find in Pikesville!

Somehow, though, he knew that what the carpenter was saying was absolutely right. He looked at the little boy, and the boy was looking at him. His eyes, Jerold's eyes, were pleading. These messages came from that little boy. Jerold thought of the text messages: *Help me. Please help. Help me. Come home.*

Jerold looked into the boy's eyes again. They seemed to cry out for help. They were so innocent and so young. Jerold remembered being seven. He started to remember what it was like to love and not to have to think about it. Yes, Jerold began to remember.

"Okay," he said, "I'd like your help. I want to help him, err, me. What do we do?"

The carpenter laughed and bounced the boy on his shoulder.

"I was hoping you'd say that. Come with me. We've got lots of work to do."

𝄞 𝄞 𝄞

Mrs. Woods sat down at her desk, opposite Darcy. She held a piece of paper in her hand.

"Honey, Joe Volker was one of the most important and well-known people in the Tri-County area. I remember him very well. He died in a fire about ten years ago, and we have really missed him. I was just telling Alberta about Joe just last week."

Darcy had about a hundred questions, and it seemed to her that Mrs. Woods could spin a good, long story. She tried to cut it off.

"Well, what happened to him, and what can you tell me about his family? His son is here."

69

"Now hold on just a minute, young lady. Don't get ahead of yourself and don't interrupt me," Mrs. Woods retorted. "I'll get to that. You and I just met and I'd hate for our first meeting to take a bad turn."

Darcy gulped, believing that this lady meant business. For a quick moment she felt like a little girl again, being scolded by her mother. Mrs. Woods just laughed, though, and that eased the tension. She patted Darcy's suddenly nervous hands.

"Relax baby. Now, back to what you asked me. Joe Volker did a lot for this town. He sure did."

She paused and then said, "You say his son is here, huh?"

"Yes ma'am He's looking for something at the old house right now. I really don't know what we're looking for or why we're here. I'd appreciate any help you can give me."

Mrs. Woods smiled again and took Darcy's hand this time.

"I want to help you, dear. I think I can, too. I've got the death certificate right here. You'll see that he died in the fire. Check out the cause of death. I think you'll find that interesting. Smoke inhalation. From there, your search should continue at the county library just down the street here. You go there, ask for Mabel. I'll call her. She'll help you find the old newspaper articles you need."

Mrs. Woods stood, so Darcy did, too. She clasped Darcy's hand in her own.

"Go on now, honey. The library is just down the road. I'll call Mabel."

Darcy left Mrs. Woods's office and walked down the marble staircase. She wasn't sure what she'd find at the library, but at least it was a start. Maybe now she would find out something that would help Jerold. Perhaps she would even find out something about Jerold himself.

$ $ $

Jerold followed the carpenter down the hall and back into the living room, which was still as burned and black as it had been when Jerold had entered. The carpenter, though, was not staying in the house. He went out the front door and into the driveway. Jerold followed him. He was surprised to notice that outside were a beautiful blue sky and soft green grass. A gentle breeze was blowing through the trees. The leaves shook gently. It was nothing like the early fall day in which he and Darcy had arrived. It was, in a word, a perfect day.

"Uh, when I came in the house earlier it was late September. It was nice, but it wasn't anything like this. What's going on?"

"Where I'm from, everything is perfect."

Jerold furrowed his brow.

"I guess," he said, not sure what else to say.

The carpenter laughed as he stopped by the broken stone wall lining the driveway. He set the little boy down next to the wall. The boy seemed content to just sit there and watch. He hadn't said anything; he just continued to clutch the teddy bear.

"This is where we start. We need to stack these stones and rebuild this wall. There's a wheelbarrow in the garage, and some cement. There are plenty of stones. Let's get to work."

The carpenter began to collect the stones that had fallen from the wall. He seemed to expect Jerold to get the wheelbarrow and cement, so Jerold shrugged his shoulders and went to the garage. He brought out the wheelbarrow and bag of cement, then fetched a bucket of water and he and the carpenter made cement. They took the trowels and began reforming the wall. Jerold thought it odd that they were going to work on rebuilding the old place. He mentioned that to the carpenter, who just waved him off.

"You just work."

Jerold found it felt good to work with his hands and actually see progress. It had been such a long time since he had been given the opportunity to do something like this. Though he thought it was strange, he liked it. As they worked, though, Jerold thought of Darcy.

"I don't want to be out of line, but I told Darcy I'd come to the house and then get her later. She's at the courthouse. I don't know what to tell her, or how much time it will take us. What am I supposed to do about her?"

The carpenter continued working.

"Don't worry about the time. It's of no concern to us."

Jerold pondered this for a second and then threw himself into working with stones and cement. He was happy not to have to think; he just wanted to do something. He worked right next to the carpenter and the seven-year-old sat by them. Occasionally the boy went for more water, and every now and then, the carpenter let him set the stones on the cement. He seemed content. They finished the first wall along the drive in what seemed like no time at all. The carpenter moved to the second wall. Jerold followed him. As they started stacking stones, the carpenter spoke.

"Jerold, you need to know some things if you want to help him," he said, nodding to the boy, who had gone off to collect more stones from the pile.

"Okay," Jerold replied, "I'm willing. What do we do?"

"We keep working," the carpenter said. "I want to talk to you. There are some things you need to know. Jerold, you need to understand something about your mom and dad. The night your mother died, your parents were together in her hospital room."

Jerold was working on stones and cement, but in his mind he could see his mom in her hospital bed. It was spooky how he could actually see it as the carpenter talked about it. There were tubes running from several different machines. Each one of the tubes was pumping some kind of liquid into her body. He saw his dad sitting in the chair next to her hospital bed.

The carpenter continued, "Your mom was not feeling well at all; in fact, the end was near. She knew it, and so did your dad. They spoke to one another that night, Jerold. You need to hear what they said."

Jerold miraculously was able to hear in his mind the conversation between his dad and mom that night...

"Ruthie, I don't know if I'll be able to go on without you. I've known this was coming, but somehow, it seems so unreal. I love you. You know that. You're the best thing that ever happened to me. Ruthie, what am I going to do?"

Jerold saw his dad drop his head onto his mom's bed and just sob. From the anguish on her face, it was obvious that his mom was in great pain. It was unnerving for Jerold to watch. He had never before seen anything like this...

"What the--How can I-- I don't think--" his words came out in bursts of incomplete thoughts. The carpenter seemed to understand.

"Jerold," he said calmly, "it's all right. Just listen..."

"Joe," his mom spoke in a voice barely above a whisper. "You gotta pull yourself together. I don't know how much time we have left, but I don't want you going to pieces."

Jerold watched as his dad straightened in his chair and wiped his eyes.

His mom continued, "Joe, you've got to be strong for the kids. You've got to remind them that I love them. You've got to raise them to achieve their dreams. I know it's not fair. I guess life isn't fair; but, Joe, when I'm gone, it's up to you."

His dad interrupted, "I can't. Ruthie, I know I can't. I've failed so much. You know I failed in that job in Louisville. It's my fault we're stuck in this stupid little town. I wanted so much more for you and the kids. I'm so sorry, Ruthie. It wasn't supposed to be like this. I failed the kids and now I've failed you!"

His mom replied with all the resolve she had in her, "Joe, that's not true. You are not a failure. You're the best man I know. Joe, you have to do it. I know you're a strong man. You're the strongest man I've ever met. I love you. This is hard, I know, for both of us. You must be strong for Janice and Jerold. They're going to need you. Now listen to me. I know you know this, but hear me out. Janice is going to need to know that you love her, but don't spoil her. Don't let her wrap you around her finger. Be strong with her. She's a good girl and will make us both proud. Just don't be too easy on her. I know you will want to be easy, so be careful. Jerold is a good little boy. He has a lot of love to give. Love him and let him grow up just like his daddy. He looks up to you and wants to be like you."

His dad, with tears streaming down his face, said, "I'll try, dear. I will. I'll be there for the kids and I'll raise 'em right. I will."

Jerold watched this scene with glassy-eyed fascination. The carpenter continued to tell the story and the scene changed in Jerold's mind. His mother was no longer talking. In fact, she was no longer breathing. The lines were flashing straight across the heart machine. Jerold knew that his mom had just died. He noticed the look of peace on her face. He also saw his dad. There were no tears in his eyes now, just a steely look. The doctor was in the room with him.

"Mr. Volker, I am so sorry. She was a wonderful person and a great fighter. I know you know that. I will pray for you and your kids."

"Thanks, doc," his dad said in almost a whisper. "Do you mind if I have a few minutes alone here with her?"

"That's no problem. Let me know when you're ready.

The doctor left the little hospital room and Jerold watched as his dad sat beside his mom's body.

"Ruthie, I promise I will do my best. I will never let the kids forget you. I will try to raise them like you want. I'll be tough. I promise. I won't let you down. Not again. I love you…"

Jerold would have liked to see a little more, but the scene dissolved, and he was staring again at a stone he had just lathered with concrete.

Jerold was deeply touched by what he had seen, but any attempt at putting it into words was failing him. He simply looked at the carpenter in amazement. The carpenter put a stone in place.

"Before I explain what all this means, there's something else you need to see. This takes place just after you left for college. Do you remember? You had a fight with your dad. He wanted you to go to Louisville right away. He would hear nothing of you staying around Pikesville for a girl. You wanted to stay, but he didn't understand. You went to Kathy's house, hoping she would understand, but she didn't. No one did. So, you left. I want you to know what happened here after you were gone."

Jerold placed the last stone in place as the carpenter spoke. In his mind he saw a gray, rainy day. He saw his dad at the cemetery next to the church in town, standing by a grave site—his mother's. Jerold heard his dad talking…

"Ruthie, I don't think I've done very well. I tried; I want you to know that."

Tears were choking his dad's words.

"It's been two years," he paused and choked up once

again before he continued, "and I haven't heard from Janice. I tried to be tough, like you said, but I did it wrong. I was too hard and too unfeeling. I knew it as it happened, but I couldn't stop. All I could think of was that she had to finish college. She had her momma's brains and there was no way I would let her run off and get married. I'm sorry, honey. She left, and I don't think she's coming back."

He bowed his head as he said, "I failed her, too, dear. I know it."

There was a pause as Jerold's dad simply stood by the grave.

Then his dad spoke quietly, "I did my best with Jerold. I tried to make him tough. I tried to instill in him the will to succeed. I hope I did, Ruthie. I'm afraid I might have squelched some of his loving. I didn't mean to, I really didn't. I just couldn't let him wither away after you died. He had to be strong. I know you said he wanted to be like me; but, Ruthie, I couldn't let that happen. I failed, but I wanted to make sure my son didn't. I didn't want him to know failure. I tried. I really tried."

Jerold watched as his dad put some flowers down on the grave. He knelt and said a little prayer, then stood. There was resolve in his eyes.

"Yes, dear," he said, "I'll keep on praying. I will write to Janice. I'll do my best to reach her and keep up with Jerold, too, if I can. I'll see you again, dear. Remember, I love you…"

"I don't think I ever saw my dad pray," Jerold said to the carpenter as the scene vanished.

"Your dad prayed a lot after you left," the carpenter

said.

"Did he ever get things straight or right, do you know?" Jerold inquired. "I never knew he thought of himself as such a failure."

"I'm sure he did," the carpenter answered.

The carpenter stood and Jerold was shocked back into the reality that was. He was standing in the driveway of what seemed to be his old house. The carpenter was wiping dry cement off of his hands. He handed a rag to Jerold, as the seven-year-old sat on the grass beside them and watched.

"What's it all about?" Jerold asked, breaking the silence.

"Jerold," the carpenter answered, "this is about you understanding. It's about you having insight into why things happened in your life."

Jerold thought for a moment. His mind was racing. All he had seen was mixing with what he had hidden deep inside of him, and it seemed to clash.

"So," Jerold finally said, "because I understand what happened to my dad and how hard it was for him, I'm supposed to say how he raised us wasn't his fault. I'm supposed to feel sorry for him?"

Jerold did not say this in anger as much as he just made a simple inquiry. To be angry, you had to care. He had long since quit caring about what had happened here. He did not think his father had ever done anything wrong as a dad. What happened was simply that: what happened. It wasn't perfect, that was certain. His dad had made some mistakes and they were not a close family. They weren't really a family at all. That was that.

It seemed, though, that this carpenter was pushing Jerold to consider understanding why things had ended up like this. He had no interest in doing so.

"Jerold," the carpenter calmly replied, "understanding doesn't mean condoning. Your dad made some mistakes. He did not do everything right; he handled some things well and some things badly. He came to understand that and regret it. He did drive Janice away, and he toughened you so much you forgot how to feel. Yes, he did those things. Understanding why those things happened in no way excuses them. But it does give you an insight. Understanding comes before forgiving."

"Forgiving?" Jerold exclaimed. "There's no way. We haven't been a family. That's just the way it is. I haven't talked to Janice for years. I hardly talked to Dad after I left Pikesville. It was what he wanted and how we were raised. I wasn't even here when he died. Hey, I'm not really mad, but I just don't care. You have to care to forgive."

The carpenter smiled again.

"Yep," he said, "you do."

With that he picked up the seven-year-old and carried him into the house.

"Come on, Jerold, we've got more work to do."

Chapter Seven

Darcy found the library just as Mrs. Woods had said. When she walked up the concrete steps and opened the door, she knew right away she was in a library by that unmistakable old book smell. She walked to the front desk, where a young lady sat next to the phone.

"Uh," she said, "excuse me. Can you tell me where I might find a Mabel?"

"You mean Mabel McCaffrey?" the girl asked.

"I suppose so," Darcy replied.

"Let me call her for you."

In just a few moments, Mrs. Mabel McCaffrey appeared.

"Just how can I help you, ma'am?" she asked.

"I was sent here by Mrs. Woods," Darcy began.

"Oh," Mabel interjected, "you're the girl Eleanor sent down. Yes. She called me. Come with me; I know what you're looking for."

Darcy followed as Mabel led her to the back of the small library. She had her sit at a table as she brought out several old newspaper copies.

"Before you read these, though, let me give you a brief history."

Darcy listened intently.

"Joe and Ruth Volker came to Pikesville a long time ago. Joe had been a big shot executive in Louisville, but he lost his job. He came here to work in the bank. When they started, they didn't have much, but Ruthie made it work and they did a great job with their kids. She got sick, though, and when she died the family crumbled. Joe continued to work. Even though his family had fallen apart, Joe worked hard. He became vice-president of the bank. He made a good salary, for here, anyway, and he saved his money. At the end of his life he had quite a bit. You need to know that as you start reading."

With that, she handed Darcy the articles. She gasped as she read the first one.

"Is this true?" she exclaimed.

"Yes," Mabel answered. "It's all true. Just keep reading."

§ § §

Jerold followed the carpenter into the house. The carpenter set the seven-year-old down as he moved to the kitchen, and the seven-year-old took the teddy bear to one of the bedrooms in the hall. Jerold had so many questions and so few answers. Who was this carpenter and how did he know so much about Jerold and his family? Why was he bringing up the past and those things? Jerold had a lot he wanted to discuss with this fellow. He didn't get the chance, however; the carpenter was ready to work.

"Jerold, there are some two-by-fours in the back. We're going to need them to repair the kitchen ceiling and walls. I cut them earlier today, so they're ready. I'll start knocking out this burned stuff while you and the boy get the new wood ready."

The seven-year-old stood next to Jerold. He waited. The more Jerold thought about this whole thing, the more he thought he'd snapped. The carpenter began knocking out blackened and burned wood. Jerold shrugged. He might as well make the best of it.

"All right," he said to the boy, "let's go."

The boy said nothing.

They went to the back yard. Jerold was startled seeing it again after such a long time. The rope was frayed, but the old tire swing still hung there. Jerold looked at it longingly, remembering the good times. His mind went back to a warm, spring Saturday afternoon. The sun was shining brightly and a gentle breeze tickled the leaves on the trees. Jerold and Janice were in this backyard playing.

"Jerold," eight-year-old Janice called out to him as she jumped on the tire, "push me."

He grabbed the tire and pulled it back as far as he could. He then ran as fast as he could, pushing the swing. He ducked as Janice's feet came back over his head. She squealed with glee. Jerold watched in his mind's eye as he stood behind his sister, pushing her higher and higher. It was fun. He could see himself laughing.

He was brought back from this pleasant memory by a tug on his hand. The seven-year-old was pulling him toward the wood pile.

"Okay," Jerold said, "let's get to it."

Jerold and the seven-year-old began collecting the wood to repair the kitchen. They made several trips, carrying in armloads of two-by-fours. As they stacked them in the living room, the carpenter worked. He had already removed the burned and broken pieces; now he was replacing them with good, solid studs. When Jerold and the seven-year-old had brought in the last of the wood, the carpenter spoke.

"Jerold, why don't you take this hammer and help me in the kitchen?"

He looked to the seven-year-old and said, "Thanks. You can hand us the wood as we need it."

Jerold took the hammer and began working. He wasn't an experienced carpenter and it was clear that he was not nearly as skilled as this stranger. He did the best he could, though. The carpenter didn't seem to mind his lack of expertise. In fact, he seemed to enjoy showing Jerold how to do it. They had worked for what seemed like half an hour when the carpenter spoke.

"Jerold, I want to talk some more."

"I thought you would," Jerold answered as he drove a nail into the sheetrock they were replacing on the newly built wall frame. "I have a lot of questions, too."

"Okay, Jerold," the carpenter said, "fair enough. What's on your mind?"

Jerold was taken aback by the carpenter's openness. He didn't quite know how to start.

"All right," he stammered, "just who are you and how do you know all this stuff?"

The carpenter smiled and replied, "Jerold, I think you know who I am. I think it has been so long that you don't recognize me, but you know. I've known you and your family for a long time. I was there when your mom got sick and when Janice left."

Jerold continued working, but his mind was on what this carpenter said.

"Why are you doing this?" Jerold finally said, barely above a whisper.

The carpenter continued to work as he replied, "Jerold, I've been asked to help you. I'm here because I care and so do others."

That was too much for Jerold. Emotions that had been bottled up in him for a long time began to leak out. He paused from nailing sheet rock to wipe his eyes with a rag. The carpenter watched. After a few minutes, he spoke.

"Jerold, you never came back to Pikesville after you left that day, did you?"

"Nope," Jerold answered. "I never wanted to, really."

"I get that," the carpenter replied. "You never saw your dad again. Why?"

Jerold had been thinking about that ever since he had seen what took place at the hospital and cemetery.

"I suppose there isn't a good reason. I was busy at college and he seemed to think that was fine. My scholarship money covered tuition. He sent a few checks that first year and, we wrote and talked a few times. After that, I got more into school and doing well. I even started making my own spending money. He, we, just

talked and wrote less until it was nothing. Excelling in school became the most important thing. Life outside of Pikesville was fast and interesting. I liked it; it made me feel good. After a while, I just stopped thinking about Dad or Pikesville at all. I didn't invite him to any of my college graduations. I don't think he would've come anyway; we didn't need each other anymore."

The carpenter listened as they worked on the walls.

"What about Janice?" he asked after a few minutes.

Jerold winced. It wasn't a subject he particularly wanted to discuss.

"What about her?" he retorted.

"I was wondering whether you had tried to contact her over the years," the carpenter replied.

Jerold frowned and answered, "I missed Janice at first. I wished she had been around for my last few years of high school. She never saw our state championship in football. She didn't come to my graduation. I understood why. She ran off to be with Tony. She went to the community college and got her nursing degree, I guess. She married Tony the year I graduated, but Dad and I didn't go to the wedding. I don't think we were invited. I knew that infuriated Dad, but I didn't expect to see her and I didn't."

"Did you ever try to reach her?" the carpenter asked.

"Nope," Jerold replied. "She had her life and I had mine. She made her choices and I had to do the same. No hard feelings. Shoot. No feelings at all."

Jerold paused for just a moment, reflecting upon the discussion.

"Patrisse, my secretary, has tried to get me to talk with

her. I suppose Janice tracked me down in Cincinnati and called her. I never take the calls, and I don't return them, either. I just don't know what to say. We've gone our separate ways. We have different lives. I hope she's happy. I do. We're not close, that's all."

They continued to rebuild the walls and ceiling of the kitchen.

"Jerold, I think you ought to know a little about Janice and what happened after you left," the carpenter said. "It's important."

Jerold sighed. He had already encountered more than he imagined he would in Pikesville. He also knew, though, that this carpenter would not relent.

He took another piece of sheetrock, fitted it to the studs and began nailing. Without looking at the carpenter, he spoke, "Go ahead."

"Jerold, after you left for school, your dad continued working at the bank. He wrote to Janice every week after she left. For almost three years she didn't reply. He knew she was in Eddyville, had gone to community college and married Tony. Many times he tried to let her know he had made a mistake, to apologize and start another relationship. There was a lot of hurt on Janice's part, and a lot of pride, but your dad never quit caring."

Jerold interrupted, "She was in Eddyville! That's only a few miles from here. Why didn't he go see her?"

The carpenter continued, "He did go to Eddyville. If he could have, he would have walked up to her to speak, to plead. He wanted to, but he didn't. He kept his distance. After a while, he stopped going. Sometimes pain, anger and fear create a gulf that's hard to bridge."

Jerold just grunted an assent. The carpenter pressed ahead.

"About fifteen years ago, Jerold, something happened that changed things. Janice got pregnant. She and Tony were going to have a baby. It was a sobering moment for Janice. She remembered her momma and her daddy. She and Tony talked about it a lot, and they decided it was time to reach out. They wanted their child to know about Grandma and have a grandpa. It wasn't a dramatic moment when Janice came home, but it was significant."

As the carpenter spoke, Jerold began to see a cool, gray day. The leaves of the trees were clustering in the driveway. Janice was about six months pregnant as she got out of her car and walked slowly to the front door of 203 Cambridge. Jerold saw her as she took a deep breath and then knocked on the door. There was a pause before the door opened, then a moment of awkward silence. Janice spoke...

"Daddy," she said, "it's me. Can I come in?"

Jerold saw his father at the door. He was slightly bent over, and what hair he had was gray. He wore old khaki pants and a dress shirt. His glasses were down on his nose. He was still proud, but it was clear that the years had taken their toll on this man. Jerold watched him as he looked at Janice. His dad gulped and spoke.

"Oh my goodness!" he exclaimed in a raspy voice. "It can't be! Janice, oh, Janice, yes. Come in. Come in."

Jerold watched as his expectant sister walked into the house. She sat down in the living room and Jerold could hear them talking.

"Janice," his dad said, "I'm so happy to see you. You can't know how long I've waited for this day. I want you to know how sorry I am."

Janice interrupted him.

"Daddy, I think we both have things for which we're sorry. That's not important now, is it? I came home because, well, I'm going to have a baby. Tony and I are-- wait-- maybe I should tell you about Tony and me..."

"Oh I would love that," his dad said. "I know you and Tony are married. I know you're a nurse. I've tried to keep up with what you're doing."

Janice smiled and said, "That's just like you, Dad. Well, then you know that Tony and I have been getting along great. In just a little while, I'm going to have our first child. I thought it was time for our baby to know Grandpa and a little about Grandma, too."

The scene changed in Jerold's mind as the carpenter continued the story. Jerold was back in the living room again, but this time there was a Christmas tree in the corner. It was decorated with a few bulbs and blinking lights. Jerold could see snow on the ground as he glanced out the window. Music came softly from a radio on the kitchen counter. Jerold could see his dad in the living room, sitting in his favorite chair, a recliner. Jerold saw Janice sitting on the couch next to a strong, muscular young man he assumed was Tony. Two children, a boy and a girl, were excitedly opening presents on the living room floor. Jerold heard Janice speaking first.

"Martha Ruth, Joey, this present is from Grandpa," she said as she handed each of them a box wrapped in red and green paper.

"Oh, boy!" Martha Ruth exclaimed as she ripped open the paper, "it's a doll! It is just the one I wanted." She clutched it to her chest. "Thank you, Grandpa," she said as she ran and jumped into his lap.

"Wow!" Jerold heard the little boy say. "This is awesome," he continued as he pulled a dump truck out of the box. "Thanks, Grandpa," he called out as he joined his sister in his lap.

Jerold watched as his dad held Martha Ruth and Joey, his grandchildren. Jerold could tell that Janice had been visiting with and caring for their dad. His clothes were new. His hair was still gray, but it was cut and combed. Looking into his dad's eyes as he held the two kids, Jerold could see a spark of joy and happiness.

He interrupted the carpenter.

"So my sister has two kids."

"Yep," the carpenter answered. "Martha Ruth, named for Tony's and Janice's mothers, and Joey named for---"

"My dad," Jerold stated flatly.

"He loved those kids and they brought him great joy the last few years of his life."

"Good," Jerold replied, though not too convincingly.

They finished the sheetrock and began cleaning up. The carpenter continued the story and Jerold was back in the house...

Janice was standing over a bed, their dad's bed. He looked even older, and his thin gray hair was uncombed. Janice had just finished taking his blood pressure.

"Well, Daddy," she said, "it's still a little high. I'll get the doctor to increase the medicine. How are you feeling?"

Jerold watched as their dad sighed.

"Not so good, kiddo," he answered. "I know it's not going well."

He started to describe his condition, but Janice cut him off.

"Now, Daddy," she said, "I know what the prognosis is. I'm the nurse, you know. But you're a strong guy. You can fight this. You've got it in you. I'll be here to help. You can't get discouraged."

"I'm not, honey," he answered, "but I'm realistic. I know what I've got. I know that sooner or later, it'll get me. But I want to talk to you."

"Okay," she said as she sat down, "what's on your mind?"

"Janice," he began, "I want you to know how much I've cherished these last few years. You, Tony and the kids have made my life wonderful. Martha Ruth is a sweet young lady. She reminds me of you and your momma. I know that your momma is proud. Little Joey is such a fine boy. He's got his daddy's looks and his momma's heart. I'm proud of you, kiddo."

Jerold saw tears in his sister's eyes.

"Janice," he continued, "I want you to know I'm thankful that you and I could be close. After all these years, nothing is more important. I know I did a lot of things wrong when your mom died. I drove you away. That fall day you came home was one of the happiest days of my life. Janice, I'm glad you and I are close again, but your brother…"

Jerold watched as Janice interrupted him.

"I'm trying, Daddy, I am," she said.

Jerold watched as his dad closed his eyes.

"Thank you, baby," he finally said.

Jerold watched as there was a moment or two of silence. Then his dad spoke again.

"Oh, yeah," he said, "please have Tony check the wiring in the kitchen. I know there's a short in there somewhere."

"I will, Daddy," Janice answered.

Jerold watched as Janice pulled the sheet up to their father's chin. She held his hand as he fell asleep...

Jerold sat down by the dwindling stack of two-by-fours, and put his head in his hands. The carpenter's stories were taking their toll on him. The carpenter continued with one last story about Janice...

He saw another cold, clear, wintry day. Janice and Tony were standing in the church cemetery. He could see little Martha Ruth and Joey holding hands. They were standing by a pile of fresh dirt, and Jerold didn't need to look at the headstone to know what had happened.

"You know, honey," a masculine voice spoke, "he's at peace now and he's with your momma. He looked forward to this day."

Jerold heard his sister speak, choked by tears.

"I know, Tony. I know. That's not why I'm crying. I just want him to know he wasn't a failure. He did so much for so many people. Martha Ruth and Joey adored him. He meant so much to me. I want him to know that. I wish I could reach Jerold."

Before she could finish, Tony squeezed her hand and she broke down. She buried her head into Tony's shoulder and wept...

Jerold was jolted back into reality when a hammer was thrust into his ribs. It was the seven-year-old, handing him the hammer he must've dropped while listening. The carpenter grinned.

"Hey," he said, "we're about finished. Don't quit working."

The carpenter then moved into the hall. Jerold followed. He had many questions.

"So," he finally said, "I guess the wiring in the kitchen never got fixed right, huh?"

The carpenter shook his head.

"Nope," he said, "It didn't. Tony never really had a chance. The fire broke out that night. It started as an electrical fire in the kitchen and spread to the living room while your dad slept. In just a few minutes this old house was blazing; the smoke was awful. Your dad never woke up. He died in his sleep."

Jerold looked away.

"Well," he said, "I guess that's the way to go. He didn't suffer."

"Not at the end," the carpenter said. "Not like you have."

Jerold grimaced.

"What do you mean by that?" he asked.

"Jerold, your dad and sister found love and joy through understanding and forgiveness. They had something special; something you've never had."

"I've never wanted it," Jerold shot back angrily. "I still don't."

"I see," the carpenter replied. "You're angry."

"I guess," Jerold spat back as he forcefully yanked a

burned two-by-four out of its place in the wall.

"Then there's more to do," the carpenter replied. "Let's get back to it."

Chapter Eight

*I*t took Darcy less than twenty minutes to read through the stack of articles Mabel had brought out for her, and she was stunned by what she read.

"Mrs. McCaffrey," she said as she completed the last one, "can I get you to make some copies of these? I know Jerold is going to want to read this."

"I knew you'd say that, so I've already made copies of all of them for you. Eleanor said Joe's boy was back in town. Here. Take them. I hope they help."

"Thank you," Darcy said as she took Mabel's hand. "Thank you so much."

§ § §

Jerold and the carpenter continued working in the hall. The seven-year-old continued to help, bringing wood and nails as was needed. Nothing much was said for a while until they had replaced much of the sheetrock and baseboards. The work was hard and tedious, but as far as Jerold was concerned, it was better than talking. He'd heard more already than he bargained for when he decided to come back to Pikesville. At this point, he wanted to finish, whatever that meant, and get out. The carpenter nailed the baseboard next to the bathroom and sat and looked at Jerold. Sweat stained the gray t-shirt he was wearing.

"Hey, we're getting this old house fixed up pretty nice, don't you think?"

Jerold nodded and answered, "Yeah, I guess so. I'm not sure why we're doing it, though."

The carpenter smiled and shook his head.

"Jerold, you are as stubborn as a Missouri mule!"

He picked up another handful of nails and began working on the baseboard extending down the hall.

"We're fixing it up for you. This whole thing is for you."

Jerold smirked and made a noise that caused both the carpenter and the seven-year-old to look.

"If that's so, then we're wasting our time. I don't care. Don't you get it? If this is supposed to be my heart, then fixing it up just isn't worth it."

The seven-year-old and the carpenter both looked sadly at Jerold as he spoke. This tempered his anger a little.

"Hey, don't get me wrong. I appreciate what you're trying to do. At least I guess I do. I'm happy for Janice and I'm glad she and my dad were able to patch things up. It's just too late for me. I don't care anymore."

The carpenter turned away from working on the base-boards to address Jerold.

"You don't care, huh," he stated a bit bluntly. "I don't believe that, Jerold. I think you do care. You care a whole lot more than you're willing to admit. You're hurt and you're angry, so you don't want to go there, but you do care."

Jerold put down his hammer and stared at the carpenter.

"That's crazy. You don't know what I'm thinking and you don't know what's going on inside of me."

Even as he said it, though, Jerold winced. He wasn't so sure that this carpenter didn't know, but he pressed ahead anyway.

"You're wrong," Jerold exclaimed.

"Am I?" the carpenter asked. "What is it you're angry about? Let's talk about it."

Before Jerold could answer, the carpenter started talking.

"Jerold, remember when you were seven and you heard the news about your mom having cancer?"

Jerold saw himself at seven years old, in his bedroom, lying on the bed with the baseball bedspread. He had been crying. His mother entered the room...

"Jerold, what's the matter, honey? Why are you crying?"

The seven-year-old Jerold lay on the bed with his head hidden in his pillow.

"Come on, Jer," his mom implored, "tell your mom."

The little boy looked up and Jerold saw anger in his tear-stained face.

"I don't want you to leave," he finally cried out. "It's not fair. Don't go! Please don't go."

Jerold saw a look of sadness in his mother's eyes.

"Jerold, it's going to be all right. I have to go. Your

daddy and I talked to you about that, remember?"

Jerold watched as the seven-year-old began to cry and bury his face again.

"But it's not fair, Mom. I don't want you to go. Please."

"Honey, I know it isn't. I don't know why things happen like this. I want you to know that I love you and I always will. You will be all right. I promise…"

Jerold watched as his mother consoled the seven-year-old. He could vaguely remember the scene being played out in his mind. In an instant he was back in the hall looking at the carpenter and the seven-year-old once again.

"Jerold," the carpenter said, "your mom did go, didn't she? You were mad. You didn't want her to leave, but she did. Everything wasn't all right."

"That's stupid," Jerold shot back, his anger rising. "Everything was okay. She didn't have a choice. She got sick! She couldn't help it! It wasn't her fault."

Jerold angrily got up and walked quickly down the hall, past the bathroom to the bedroom. He paused at the bedroom door as he heard the carpenter speak.

"It's okay to be angry. I understand that. I also know you're mad at your dad, huh?"

Before he could respond he recognized the warm day in May. He was at Kathy's house. He knew what was going to happen…

"Kathy, I'll come back to visit, I promise. This is an opportunity to make some money and get some experience for college. It doesn't mean that we're through, though. Maybe you can visit me in Louisville. It will work."

Kathy shook her head.

"No it won't. You'll be a hundred miles away in Louisville and I'll be here. We won't have any time together. You'll meet other people and new girls, lots of them. If you go, Jerold, we've got to end it."

Jerold felt frustration building inside of him.

"Listen, Kathy, it won't be like that. I won't let it. I'll call you."

"Jerold," she said emphatically, "you have to make a choice. If you go to Louisville, then we're through. There's no other way."

"Kathy," Jerold practically begged.

"No," she said with tears in her eyes.

In a few minutes Jerold saw himself leave Kathy's house. He saw that as he left, Kathy went to her bedroom and cried. He was no longer in a relationship and his emotions were bubbling inside of him. Her final words were still ringing in his ears. *No, Jerold! If you leave, we're through.* What choice did he have? Jerold was becoming more irritated and angry. He got into his car, slammed the door and started the engine, and the tires squealed as he pulled out of Kathy's driveway. Jerold felt like a person without a home. His dad had made it clear that there was no way he was staying; his future was elsewhere. He had to go to Louisville. Jerold wasn't sure, but he thought he might love Kathy. He had not thought his dad would understand, and he hadn't. He had hoped Kathy would understand his situation, but she didn't either. As he drove down Main Street, he felt lost and alone. Before going home he decided to drive by the school once more. He parked the car in the lot next to the football field, and the loose gravel crunched under his feet as he got out. The football field was empty and deserted. Jerold stood at the chain link fence surrounding the field as he remembered all the good times he'd had out there. People loved him for what he did on that field. Out there he did not have any worries. What he wouldn't give to be out there once again.

The emotions boiling in him converged at that moment and Jerold ran. He wasn't running away from anything, really, and yet, in a lot of ways, he was. Across the football field, past the visiting team bleachers to the farm land next to the school, he ran. At the creek that bordered the farm he fell and buried his face in his hands.

"This isn't fair! Why do I have to do this? I don't want to go! I need to go! Tell me. Why? Why can't Kathy understand? Why can't my dad realize?"

Jerold poured out his feelings and emotions. The gentle gurgling of the creek and the singing of the birds were drowned out by every "why" question Jerold could pose. He poured out his heart into the solitude of that creek, but there was no response. After several minutes of pleading, Jerold simply got up and wiped his eyes with his sleeve. There were no answers here. He walked slowly across the farm and the football field to his car, and then it was a short drive down Main Street and back home...

"Jerold," the carpenter said softly, "you cried out at that creek. You were angry."

Jerold looked at the carpenter with a hardened expression.

"It didn't matter whether I was angry or not. There wasn't anyone there to hear me. No one cared. It just didn't matter."

"That's not quite true, Jerold," the carpenter replied. "God was there and He heard you."

"God!" Jerold exclaimed, "That's ludicrous! God wasn't there. He doesn't care and never has. I went home, had dinner with my dad and left. That's what happened. No one knew about that creek. No one knew how I felt and no one cared. That's it!"

The carpenter bowed his head before speaking.

"I saw you at the creek. I saw you pour your heart out. I saw the pain and the anguish. I heard you."

"That's not true," Jerold shouted back angrily. "No one was there. I know!"

"You buried your face in your hands. You cried out because you thought you loved Kathy. You struggled because you didn't want to disappoint your dad. At the end, you wiped your eyes with your sleeve. You walked back across the farm to the football field. You stopped at the forty yard line to look at the home team bench one more time."

Jerold wasn't sure how this carpenter knew all of these things, but he had clearly been there. Jerold ignored the obvious question of how to get to the more important question, why.

"Why didn't you do something?" he demanded. "Why didn't you help me? Why did you leave me to face this by myself?"

The carpenter moved closer to Jerold and touched his shoulder.

"Good, Jerold," he said. "Get it out in the open. You *are* mad. You're mad at God."

Jerold paused for a moment to think about what the carpenter had said. Mad at God? He'd never thought of it that way; but now, for some reason, it seemed to make sense.

The carpenter continued, "Jerold, you're angry with God because you think He wasn't there for you. You think He took your mom."

As the carpenter spoke, scene after scene played in rapid succession in Jerold's mind…

A six-year-old boy kneeling beside his bed, praying, "Dear God please let my mommy get better."

There he was again, a seven-year-old, standing at the grave of his mother. Tears filled his eyes. He heard all the voices around him, but it was only noise. All he knew was that his mother wasn't coming home.

An elementary school art class was making a project for Mothers' Day. Jerold did the project and wrapped it in the pretty paper, but he knew there was no mom at home to open it.

At fourteen he was becoming a young man. Feelings and emotions were getting all mixed up and he wasn't sure what to do. He could talk to his dad, but that seemed awkward. What he really wanted to do was talk to his mom.

There he was, at sixteen, watching his sister angrily leave and his dad frantically trying to reason with her. He knew the one who could calm them wasn't going to. Mom wasn't home.

He was a man at eighteen. His dad had been carrying the weight of the family on his shoulders as much as he could, but the load was heavy. Jerold was seeking understanding but got directives. He was looking for assurance and received advice. He was reaching for his mom, but she was gone...

It occurred to Jerold, as he stood in the hall of that burned-out house at 203 Cambridge Street, that the connecting thread to all of the problems his family faced was this one truth: God did not save his mom. God had let him down. Something snapped inside of Jerold Volker, and when it did the emotions poured out.

"Yes!" he exclaimed as tears spilled freely. "Yes, I am angry. I am mad as...How could He do that? Why didn't He hear my prayer? Why did He let my mom die? There was so much hurt and so much pain after that. How could He do that? You know so much, tell me how come God did that? Why didn't you do something?"

The carpenter stood silently by Jerold as he poured out his long-held emotions. The seven-year-old sat wide-eyed at the other end of the hall.

"Jerold," the carpenter answered, "I understand. I do."

Jerold looked at him sadly. He was broken inside.

"A lot of things happen in this world that are hard to grasp. Some things we won't fully understand until we get to the next world," the carpenter continued.

"But why?" Jerold interrupted. "Why my family, and why so much pain?"

"Jerold," the carpenter answered, "God loves you and your family. He always has and always will. Sometimes

102

ugly, bad things happen to His children here, but the truth is He never stops loving them and they never go through it alone. I was here with your mom and dad. I was with Janice, and I've been with you. I know that's not the answer you're looking for, but that's the answer you need right now. You have to come out from behind the wall, take a risk and trust that someone does love you and won't leave you alone. You have to trust God, me and then others. That's how we make it through those dark times."

Jerold stood limply, leaning against the wall. The carpenter took the hammer that dangled from Jerold's hand.

"Hey, listen, why don't you let me work in here for a while and you take a break."

He pointed to the seven-year-old who was still sitting at the end of the hall.

"Why don't you guys go outside? Get some air," the carpenter said.

Jerold nodded and walked to the end of the hall. The seven-year-old took his hand. Jerold looked back and saw the carpenter walk into Janice's bedroom. He and the seven-year-old walked through the living room and into the kitchen.

"You want to go outside?" Jerold asked the seven-year-old.

The seven-year-old nodded. They stepped out of the back door and back into the bright sunshine.

Jerold shielded his eyes as he said, "Boy, it sure is bright out here."

The seven-year-old tugged at Jerold's hand, pulling

him.

"You want to swing on the tire swing?" Jerold asked as the boy pulled him that direction. "Okay, I guess it will hold you," he continued as he fingered the frayed rope.

The boy climbed up on the tire and sat, looking at Jerold. Jerold shrugged and grabbed the tire.

"Okay, hang on."

Jerold pulled the tire back as far as he could.

"Are you ready?" he asked the seven-year-old.

The boy nodded and Jerold pushed the tire as far as he could and then ducked as it flew back by him.

"Hang on tight," he called out to the seven-year-old.

For the first time since he had seen him in the closet, Jerold saw the seven-year-old smile. It made him smile, too.

"Get ready for a Mega Push," he called out to the boy as he grabbed the tire again.

Jerold gave the tire swing a "Mega Push" and the seven-year-old giggled. It was one of those involuntary squeals of glee that kids do. Jerold heard it, and he laughed, too. Inside the house, the carpenter smiled. His work was almost finished.

Chapter Nine

Jerold and the seven-year-old played for what seemed like several minutes. The seven-year-old laughed, as did Jerold. They sat on the grass under the tree and Jerold turned to him.

"Well, I suppose we ought to go back to work. What do you think?"

The seven-year-old looked up at him and smiled. Jerold put his hand on the boy's shoulder and pulled him close.

"I really had fun," he told him. "I did."

The boy smiled and climbed up on his shoulders. Jerold held the boy's hands and stood, carrying him on his shoulders. They walked to the house and Jerold ducked so the seven-year-old wouldn't bump his head.

"There you go, buddy," he told the boy as he put him down in the kitchen. "We'd better see what the carpenter needs us to do next."

The seven-year-old ran ahead of Jerold into the living room and down the hall. Jerold followed.

"Slow down a little," he called to the boy.

ʂ ʂ ʂ

Darcy ran down Main Street carrying the copies in an envelope given her by Mrs. McCaffrey. She ran up the courthouse steps, across the first floor, and up the marble staircase two steps at a time down the hall to the records office.

"Mrs. Woods!" she called out as she entered the office.

Mrs. Woods was sitting at her desk around the corner.

"Come on around, honey," Mrs. Woods called out. "I see you found what you were looking for. Well, what do you think?"

Darcy sat in the chair next to her.

"I can't believe it," she cried. "I just can't. I know Jerold doesn't know this and it's bound to change everything. I just know it will."

Mrs. Woods smiled as she said, "The truth usually does."

"What do I do now?" she said to her, believing that this woman whom she had just met would know. "I've got to tell Jerold. He has to know."

Mrs. Woods smiled. She stood and turned to get two mugs from the cabinet above her desk.

"You will, baby, you will," she said, "when the time is right."

"What do you mean?" Darcy asked.

"He'll come to get you and then you'll tell him. Until then, have some cocoa and tell me about yourself."

ʂ ʂ ʂ

Jerold reached the hall and found the carpenter standing there packing his tools.

"What's going on?" Jerold asked. "We still have more work to do, don't we?"

"Well," the carpenter replied, "I'm about finished. Why don't you take a look?"

The carpenter walked Jerold and the seven-year-old through the hall to Janice's room. When Jerold looked inside, he was stunned. Where there used to be burned, charred wood, there were now clean sheets of drywall. The ceiling was no longer falling down. They went to the bathroom next, and Jerold was shocked. It was clean. The mirror was no longer black from smoke. The walls were strong and solid. He then took Jerold and the seven-year-old to Jerold's old bedroom. It was, as it had been, painted blue with baseball curtains and bedspread. Last, he led Jerold to his dad's room. Jerold was a little reluctant to enter this room; he had been avoiding it throughout the day.

"I don't know," he said as he stopped at the doorway. "Do we need to go in here? I can take your word for it. I know you've worked here. I'm sure it's all right."

"Jerold," the carpenter answered, "I want you to see it."

"Okay," Jerold replied reluctantly.

The carpenter opened the door and he, Jerold and the seven-year-old stepped inside. Jerold was stunned to see the room was not the blackened mess he had anticipated. He didn't know why he had thought it would be. The carpenter had fixed up everything else, but it just seemed awkward to Jerold to be in the place where his dad had died. He looked around and saw that the walls had new boards. The ceiling was not burned out. The smoke damage that had been everywhere in this room was gone, and everything was clean. Jerold saw a double bed in the middle of the room and a dresser with a mirror against the wall. A night stand stood next to the bed and on it was a picture of his mother. She had to have been in high school when this picture was taken.

"This is how your dad wanted you to see this room," the carpenter told Jerold.

Jerold stepped through the door and walked to the dresser. He picked up the comb lying there. He looked into the mirror, the same mirror his dad had looked into day after day. He walked over to the night stand and picked up the picture to look at his mom, who was no more than eighteen years old and beautiful there. She had so much life to live. She had so much joy and sorrow ahead of her.

"She's beautiful," Jerold said to the carpenter and to the seven-year-old. "She sure is," the carpenter agreed.

Jerold walked back to the dresser. Behind the comb he saw another frame, a picture of his family at the Ohio amusement park, his dad with his arm around his mom, who still had her hair. They were both smiling. Janice was standing next to their dad, holding a balloon. Then Jerold saw himself, the seven-year-old, holding his mom's hand. He was laughing. Jerold remembered this day. It was a family vacation, their last one.

"That's how your dad wanted to remember you all," the carpenter said. "He kept this picture here on the dresser until the day he died. He made Janice promise to leave it here."

Jerold held the picture and motioned to the seven-year-old. The boy came close and Jerold knelt down to him. He pointed to the picture.

"Look, see. That's us, you and me. We had fun, didn't we? This is Momma and Daddy. There's Janice."

The boy nodded as he looked intently at the picture. After a few minutes, Jerold put the picture back on the dresser.

"Well," he said, "I'm glad I came in here. I didn't want to, you know. I don't know why. I've been in every room of the house except this one. I was hoping you wouldn't come in here, but I should have known better. I guess I have to say I'm really glad you did."

The carpenter smiled again.

"I'm glad you came in here, too. The truth is, though, that coming into this room wasn't my idea."

Jerold was puzzled.

"What do you mean?"

"It was his idea," the carpenter said, pointing to the seven-year-old.

The seven-year-old then stepped forward. He grabbed Jerold's hand.

"What?" Jerold asked him. "Do you have something to show me in here? What is it?"

The seven-year-old led Jerold around his dad's bed. He pulled back the covers to reveal the pillows.

"What are you doing?" Jerold asked, puzzled by the boy's strange behavior.

The seven-year-old continued to pull back the covers and lift up one of the pillows. Jerold was shocked at what was under the pillow.

"I don't believe it," he gasped.

"Jerold, he kept it with him from the day he took it from you. At the end, he held it at night. It reminded him of you and the family."

Jerold stared at the old teddy bear lying under the pillow. The seven-year-old picked up the bear and pointed it at Jerold.

"Do you want me to take it?" he asked.

The boy thrust the bear at Jerold and then walked behind the bed. He put the bear down behind the bed and walked back to Jerold. He pointed at Jerold and then pointed to the bear.

Jerold thought for a moment and then it hit him.

"It's still there, isn't it?" he asked. "The bear; it's still in the house."

The boy reached out to Jerold and he picked him up. The boy rested his head on Jerold's shoulder.

"Yep," the carpenter answered. "I think he's telling you something important."

Jerold set the seven-year-old down and knelt beside him. He looked him in the eyes and spoke to him.

"This bear is still in the house, isn't it?"

The boy nodded.

"You want me to have it, huh? You want me to have the bear?"

The boy shook his head.

"I don't get it," Jerold implored. "You don't want me to have it?"

The boy shook his head violently now.

"Okay, okay," Jerold said, calming the seven-year-old. "I'm supposed to have the bear," he started again.

The boy interrupted by nodding emphatically.

"All right," Jerold said, "but you're not the one who's giving it to me."

Again, the boy nodded.

"Okay," Jerold said, "we're getting somewhere."

He looked to the carpenter and smiled. The carpenter smiled back.

"If you're not giving it to me," he asked, "then who is?"

The seven-year-old took him by the hand and led him to the dresser. He picked up the amusement park picture and pulled Jerold down to his level. He held the picture up to Jerold and pointed. Tears filled Jerold's eyes as the seven-year-old pointed to his dad.

"My dad, our dad," Jerold stammered. "I don't know."

Jerold was at a loss for words.

The carpenter spoke for the first time in a long time, "Don't you see? Your dad wants to let you know that he understands. He wants you to know it's okay to be afraid and it's all right to love."

Jerold was still speechless. He looked into the eyes of his seven-year-old self. In them he saw innocence, joy and love. He turned to the mirror and studied his own eyes. In them were hardness, fear and bitterness. So many things he had missed and, yet, here was a chance at something better. Jerold knew this was the moment. This was his crossroads. He could leave, find Darcy and they could go back to Cincinnati, where things could go back to normal. But could they? Could they ever really be normal? Jerold couldn't imagine how. He had seen what was deep inside of him. He had received the message: this was his moment. The carpenter stood at the doorway of his dad's bedroom while the seven-year-old was holding his hand next to him. They were waiting.

"Yes," he whispered. "Yes, I want to. I want to love again. I want to live again."

Jerold sat down on the bed and the seven-year-old crawled up into his lap.

"I understand, Dad," Jerold said, "I know you had more responsibility and work than you should have had. I know that you did your best. Janice, I know why you left and I don't blame you. I know what you did when you came back. How can I ever thank you? Momma, I understand that you had to leave. I know you didn't have a choice. I know. I'm not mad anymore."

Jerold paused for a moment to look to the carpenter.

"I'm not mad at God anymore, either," he said. "I guess I was. I have been. I didn't think you cared. I didn't think I mattered. I was just a guy. So I wanted to prove everyone wrong. I wanted everyone to know I was somebody."

Jerold looked at his seven-year-old self, as he continued, "But I'm not that way now. I understand there are things I just don't get, yet."

Jerold cleared his throat.

"And I want you to know, Dad, I forgive you. I do. And I'm sorry, too. I know I haven't done the right thing, either. I'm not holding grudges anymore. I want to let it go."

He looked at the carpenter.

"Same for you," he said with a slight smile.

The carpenter walked across the bedroom and sat down on the bed next to Jerold and the seven-year-old. He put his arm around them.

"It's okay, pal, we understand. I love you."

The three of them sat in the bedroom for a few minutes, just silently taking in all that had transpired. After a few minutes, the carpenter stood. He picked up the seven-year-old as he spoke to him.

"Well, my friend, it's time for you and me to go."

Jerold was jolted by that.

"What do you mean?" he replied. "You're leaving?"

"Yep, we can't stay forever. We've got to go and so do you."

With that, he took the seven-year-old out of the bedroom and back into the hall. Jerold was bothered that he might not be seeing these two anymore.

"Are you sure? Can't you stay a little while longer? I have more questions. I need more help."

The carpenter interrupted.

"Jerold," he said, "You do have more questions and more to do. I know that. I will always be with you. You know that, too. I will be with you until the end of the world."

Jerold stood at the doorway of his bedroom as he answered, "Yeah, I know."

Jerold watched as the carpenter opened the closet door again. He set the seven-year-old back down in the closet and smiled at him. The seven-year-old sat quietly. He looked into the soft eyes of the carpenter. Jerold ran quickly into the room.

"Wait," he called out. "Wait!"

Jerold stood before the closet. It seemed like ages ago that he had first opened this door. Now he stood before his seven-year-old self. He looked into the boy's eyes, his own eyes, and was choked up. He wanted to say something to let the boy to know that everything was going to be all right; it was important that he understand that. But words failed him. The boy, though, knew what to say. He spoke for the first time.

"Thank you," he said.

The carpenter smiled and Jerold relaxed a bit. The boy waved as the carpenter closed the door.

"Well, Jerold, it's time for me to go, too."

"Are you sure?" Jerold asked him. "I'm not sure I'm ready."

"You'll be all right," the carpenter told him.

The carpenter then walked to the door of Jerold's old room.

"See you, buddy," he called to him.

Then he flicked the light switch and the room went dark. Jerold's eyes couldn't adjust, and for a while he could see nothing. When his eyes finally cleared, he looked around the room to see there were no bedspread and no curtains. He ran to the light switch and flicked it quickly, but there was no electricity. The walls were burnt and smoke-damaged. Jerold stumbled over the bed as he hurried to the closet. He threw open the door and there was nothing but dust and a few lonely hangers. Jerold took a deep breath. He stepped out of his room and back into the hall. It was blackened by soot and damaged by fire. He walked through the hall, soaking it all in. As he passed his parents' room, he had a thought. He opened the door and noticed that the fire had been really bad in here. Everything was a mess. Charred remains of furniture cluttered the room. The bed was jostled and out of place and broken glass littered the floor. Jerold went to the bed and pulled back what covers there were. Underneath a browned bed sheet, he saw a lump. He knew what it was. He reached down and picked up his teddy bear.

As Jerold walked into the living room, he felt his cell phone in his pocket: Darcy. He had nearly forgotten. He punched in her number and she answered on the first ring.

"Hello, Darce," he said.

"Jerold," Darcy told him excitedly, "I've found something. I'm here at the courthouse. You've got to see it. Come right away."

Jerold smiled.

"Okay, Darce," he answered, "I'll be there. I've got a lot to tell you, too."

Chapter Ten

Jerold walked back out onto the front porch and saw the numbers 203 attached to the side of the house. One of the screws holding the three had come loose and it hung a bit crookedly. How many times had he stood on this porch? It had only been a couple of hours since he had stepped through the front door, but it seemed like a lifetime. Certainly his life had been changed. He walked down the driveway, bordered by the falling-down rock walls. Since Jerold had been inside, the sky had turned gray and threatened rain. He started the BMW and backed out of the drive onto Cambridge Street. Main Street was just ahead. As he saw the old school building in the rear view mirror, faces of classmates and teachers filled his mind. He noticed the playground equipment was still standing, though the school had closed, and he realized the memories which filled his mind no longer tormented him.

It took only a few minutes for Jerold to reach the town square, where pulled up in front of the courthouse and parked the car. As he climbed out and shut the door, he heard a noise behind him. Darcy had been watching and was now running down the stairs to meet him.

"Jerold," she said breathlessly. "Jerold, you won't believe it!"

"Slow down, Darce," he replied. "What's got you so fired up?"

Darcy grabbed his hand and began pulling him up the stairs.

"You've got to see this," she exclaimed. "You won't believe it. You just won't."

Jerold followed Darcy up the stairs, noticing with amusement that she was taking them two at a time. She pulled open the heavy door at the top and stepped quickly inside as Jerold followed. She started down the hallway, but Jerold grabbed her. It was like trying to rein in a wild colt.

"Whoa, Darcy! Before I get completely blown over, why don't you tell me what you've been doing?"

Darcy stopped, though it was clear she wanted to get to her destination.

"After you dropped me off here, I went to the office of records and met Mrs. Woods. She's lived in Pikesville nearly all of her life. She knew your dad. I asked about his death certificate. She was able to pull that for me. It was just like Martha Miller told us. There was a fire at 203 Cambridge just over ten years ago. Your dad died in the fire. The death certificate said he died of smoke inhalation."

Jerold was puzzled and interrupted Darcy.

"It said he died of what?"

"Smoke inhalation," Darcy replied.

"Are you sure?" Jerold inquired.

"Yep," she replied, her eyes glistening. "There's more."

Jerold just shook his head.

"Mrs. Woods told me there was much more to the story than just the death certificate. She said it was the strangest thing she had ever seen. I pushed her to tell me, but she wouldn't. She said I should read it for myself and told me to go to the library. They keep old copies of the Tri-County Citizen there. She said I should check out what was written at the time of the fire and Joe Volker's death."

Jerold continued to listen intently, but it was difficult. He wanted to hear Darcy, but the encounter with the carpenter was making it hard for anything else to matter.

"So I did. I walked down to the library and found the articles. There were several, Jerold. They wrote a lot about your dad, his life and his death. It was so incredible. I got copies of all of them and I ran back to the courthouse. Mrs. Woods was kind enough to let me use a conference room. I've got all the articles there. Jerold, you won't believe it."

She took Jerold by the hand once again and yanked him up the inside stairs. When they got to the second floor of the courthouse, Darcy practically sprinted to the third office on the right. The sign on the door read in gold letters, "County Records." Under that, in smaller black letters, was the name "Eleanor Woods." Darcy pulled open the door.

"Mrs. Woods," she called out. "Mrs. Woods?"

"Yes, dear," she replied, "I see you're back."

"Yes, ma'am," she answered. "It was just like you said. Jerold is…Oh, I'm sorry. I should introduce you. Mrs. Woods, this is Jerold Volker. Jerold, this is Mrs. Woods."

"That's all right, baby. No introduction is necessary. I would recognize that boy anywhere. You look just like your daddy."

Mrs. Woods stood and, with the help of her cane, came around the desk. Jerold extended his hand, but Mrs. Woods ignored it and hugged him tightly. Normally Jerold would have found that awkward, but, for some reason, it didn't seem to bother him.

"Mrs. Woods, I take it you knew my dad."

Mrs. Woods stepped back and had a big smile on her face as she answered.

"Knew your dad?" she exclaimed. "Honey, everyone around here knew your dad." Jerold was puzzled and replied, "I don't understand."

"You will, baby," she answered. "Come on."

Mrs. Woods released Jerold and walked by him to Darcy.

"It's time, honey. Let's go."

The hall was empty as the three of them walked slowly toward the last room. The only sound came from the thwacks of Mrs. Woods' cane. The door was already open and Darcy walked in. Mrs. Woods stood at the door and ushered Jerold in.

"Right here," she told him. "Come on in, Mr. Volker. I think your lady friend has everything ready for you."

Jerold noticed the table that was covered with photocopies of four or five newspaper articles. He sat down in a chair and looked at Darcy, who was obviously anxious to share her findings. Mrs. Woods stood at the door. Before Darcy could start, she spoke: "I'll just close this door and leave you two alone for a while. Take as much time as you need, honey," she said to Darcy.

As the door closed, Darcy began excitedly.

"Jerold, start with this one," she said, taking the first article in her hand and thrusting it before him. "It's dated the day after your dad died and details what happened. Faulty wiring, most likely from the kitchen, started the fire. Neighbors and the firemen made comments. It's pretty much a news report, but I want you to read this."

She pointed at a highlighted part of the article, a quote from the volunteer fire captain. Jerold read the words and then read them again. He looked at Darcy, who read the words again aloud. "'It's the strangest thing I ever saw. The fire was bad in the main bedroom. I would have expected the victim to be badly burned, but he wasn't. It was like something protected that body. He died of smoke inhalation. I've never seen anything like it in my twenty years.'"

"Isn't that strange, Jerold?" she said. "It's hard to believe."

"Darce," he said, "I can. I know you won't get it, at least not yet, anyway, but I do."

Darcy looked like she wanted to press the point, but Jerold picked up the second article on the table. Darcy was excited.

"Jerold, that one floored me."

Jerold began reading. Darcy was quiet for a few moments as Jerold finished scanning the copy. When he finished, he looked toward her.

"Isn't that incredible? This editorial is a tribute to your dad. Jerold, he was a great man in this community. He started with virtually nothing at the bank but a job and built up quite a fortune. He started a foundation for families dealing with cancer in the Tri-County area. Did you notice that it mentioned your mom died of cancer and that your dad had it, too? He put thousands of dollars of his own money into this foundation. He was especially concerned with kids dealing with cancer. They seemed to really touch him. Did you catch the name of the foundation, Jerold? It's called "The Bear Fund." I thought that was cute, but it was also practical. Jerold, your dad's foundation not only gives money to families affected by cancer, but they give out teddy bears to the kids. Isn't that something?"

Jerold just stared at the copy of the editorial. Darcy continued.

"Did you see this, Jerold?" she asked, pointing to a particular part of the editorial. "Your sister Janice is the director of the foundation. She's a nurse at the county hospital and has connections in the medical field. I was so surprised!"

Jerold stammered, at a loss for words. Two of the other articles were compilations from regional papers about the loss of a pillar in Pikesville. The final article, from The Tri-County Citizen, was an interview with Janice. In it she talked about the foundation and her commitment to keep alive what her father was doing. It was a pleasant article and Jerold smiled when he saw his sister's picture on the front page of the paper. There was, though, an awkward part of the story when the interviewer asked Janice about her family. She spoke lovingly of her parents, her husband and children. The reporter, though, had done his homework. There was a brother. When asked about him, Janice gave a stumbling, rambling answer about being close for a while and then estranged. The answer was weak, but the reporter was kind enough to not follow up with another question.

"So, Jerold," Darcy asked, "what do you think? Amazing, huh?"

Jerold looked down at the table and cleared his throat. He reached out his hand and took hers.

"Darcy, you did great. Thank you. I didn't know any of this, I guess you know that. I can't believe you found so much in so little time."

Darcy blushed.

Jerold continued, "I need to tell you what I've been doing. When I do, I think what you've found will make sense."

Darcy looked to Jerold and replied, "Okay."

Jerold again looked down at the table. Where did he begin to describe his morning at 203 Cambridge? He decided to just tell it as it had happened.

"What I'm about to tell you is true, I swear it is. But if you don't believe me, then I won't blame you, because I'm not sure I would believe it if it hadn't happened to me. I walked into the house and it was awful. It was a terrible mess; drunks and looters had been there. I was certain I had made a mistake. First I went to the kitchen and the living room, and then I wandered down the hall into the bedroom, my old bedroom. That's where it happened."

For thirty minutes Jerold told his story and Darcy listened. Every now and then she needed a tissue to wipe her eyes. As Jerold ended the story, he squeezed her hand.

"Darce," he said, "do you believe me?"

Darcy looked down at the table and then at Jerold. This moment was an important one to them both.

"Yes, Jerold, I do. Where do we go from here? What do we do next?"

Jerold got up from the table and began collecting the copies of the newspaper articles.

"I want to keep these," he announced as he gathered them.

Darcy had the envelope Mrs. McCaffrey had given her and they placed the copies in it before they walked down the hall to the "County Records" office.

"Mrs. Woods," Jerold called out as they entered, "I want to thank you."

Mrs. Woods stood from behind her desk and embraced Jerold.

"I'm so glad you got a chance to come back here. I hope I'll see more of you."

"Yeah," he replied, "I hope so, too."

Darcy stepped out from behind Jerold.

"Mrs. Woods," she said, "thank you so much. You were so good to me."

"You're welcome, honey," she answered.

They hugged tightly. As Darcy turned away, Mrs. Woods waved to her and called out, "Good luck, baby."

Darcy waved back as they left the office. They walked

slowly down the marble staircase, through the main hall to the heavy doors. Neither of them said anything; too many things had happened in this short visit to Pikesville. The rain had stopped, but the sky was still gray and threatened more rain as they walked to the BMW.

"So, Jerold, now where do we go?"

"I've been thinking about that since we left Mrs. Woods," he answered. "If it is okay with you, I'd like to make a couple more stops today."

Darcy nodded and Jerold pulled the BMW out onto Main Street.

"If I remember right," Jerold said to her, "There's a flower shop just off of Main."

Jerold's memory was correct and in a few minutes they were in front of a little shop called, "Brown's Florist."

"Let me go in for just a second. I'll be right back," Jerold said.

"Okay," Darcy replied, "I'll just wait."

Jerold returned carrying a bouquet of fresh-cut flowers.

"Darcy," he said, "hold these for me, please."

She took the flowers and he started the car once again.

"Where are we going now?"

"A place I haven't been to for a long time," he told her.

They drove down Main, turned and were soon in the parking lot of the small Baptist church. Jerold parked the car in the newly paved lot and walked around to open Darcy's door. She stepped out carrying the flowers.

"Jerold, why are we here?"

Jerold didn't answer. He continued walking around the church to the cemetery in the back, Darcy following him. The grass was wet and a few places were muddy, so they stepped carefully. The cemetery wasn't too big and in just a few minutes Jerold stopped in front of a large headstone. Darcy started to speak, but read the stone and stopped. The name at the top was "VOLKER." She saw the other names: "Ruth" and "Joseph." Looking at Jerold, seeing his eyes welling up with tears, she handed him the flowers and he took them, knelt down and placed them in the soft earth in front of the stone. Neither of them spoke for a while. Jerold just knelt in front of the stone and Darcy rested her hand on his shoulder.

"Well, Mom," Jerold finally said, choking back tears, "I'm back. I brought you flowers. I know I haven't been here in a while. It's not like I...I just didn't...I don't know, Mom, I don't know. I'm sorry. I'm sorry. I've missed you so much."

Jerold paused and then turned to the other side of the stone.

"Dad," he said, "It's me, Jerold. I know what happened. I want you to know that. I'm sorry I wasn't here for you. I also want you to know that I am so proud of you. You touched a lot of people. You were never a failure, never." The clouds became dark and thunder rumbled in the distance. Jerold knelt at the headstone of his parents with Darcy standing by him, patting his shoulder as the rain began falling slowly. A few drops hit the stone and Darcy looked up to the gray sky.

"Jerold, a storm is coming. We'd better get in."

Jerold stood as the rain began to fall harder. Darcy

started to walk back to the BMW, but he stopped her and pulled her close. The rain poured heavily as he spoke.

"Darcy, I want you to know something."

She looked at him as the rain streaked his face.

"Darcy, I love you."

Somewhere, in the distance, between the rumbles of thunder and the flashes of lightning, a seven-year-old laughed.

Chapter Eleven

The mild fall weather ushered in a cold, snowy winter in southwestern Ohio. It had been four months since Jerold and Darcy came back from their adventure in Pikesville, and a lot had happened since then. A suburban councilman had been caught in a money laundering scandal that was making headlines. The Bengals were wrapping up another season with a chance to qualify for the playoffs. Many people throughout the state were anticipating New Year's Day and the Ohio State Buckeyes in the Rose Bowl. Freezing rain and snow filled the air, but mixed with them were excitement and anticipation. Something was happening.

Something had happened to Jerold Volker, too. He wasn't the same person he had been at the end of the summer. He was more relaxed, loose and happy. Relationships with those around him had become as important as his work. His life had taken on another dimension. Certainly he and Darcy were different. Most attributed the positive change in Jerold to the fact that he had finally worked up the courage to ask Darcy to marry him. The entire eighteenth floor of the office building had celebrated on the day after the momentous occasion. Patrisse wept with joy. Jerold was different and he needed to be. Not all that was happening was good.

The sky was clear and blue when the three of them walked into the courthouse, but it was cold and snow blanketed the ground. Jerold and Darcy walked up the steps with the young man between them. Jerold and the young man were wearing suits, and Darcy wore a navy blue dress. It seemed like the end and yet it was a beginning.

"We go to the third floor," Jerold said to Darcy and the young man as they walked in.

Darcy looked at her watch.

"Jer, we're early. I would like to visit the restroom first."

"Yeah," the young man said, "I would, too."

As they left, Jerold stood by the elevator and thought about the last few months. It had been a tough time. It had started the day Patrisse buzzed him, just after noon, to tell him she felt sick and needed to go home. That was unusual and it got worse. For the first time since Jerold had met her, Patrisse started taking sick days. She wasn't able to work as hard or as long as she had previously. She started losing weight. Jerold noticed it and spoke to her about going to the doctor. He even contacted a specialist on his own. Patrisse was irritated but grateful for his concern.

After visits to many different doctors, Patrisse got the diagnosis. She had cancer. It had gone undetected for a long time, maybe due to the fact that Patrisse, in giving to others, never really took care of herself. The doctors spoke of treatment, but no one seemed hopeful. The cancer had spread from her lungs to her liver and even to parts of her brain. It was a matter of time. That news devastated the eighteenth floor and crushed Jerold. Patrisse was his best friend. She had always believed in him. It was hard to imagine life without her. Patrisse, though, wasn't concerned about that. She had only one worry: Darrion. Jerold remembered the conversation as if it happened yesterday. ..

Patrisse was sleeping in her hospital bed. She was emaciated and tubes connected her to medicines that dulled the pain. Jerold walked in carrying a bouquet of flowers, which he set on the stand by the bed before he tapped her on the shoulder.

"Patrisse," he said, "Patrisse. It's me, Jerold."

Patrisse opened her eyes. It took a few seconds for her to focus on him and then a faint smile came to her face.

"Jerold," she whispered, "I'm glad to see you."

"How are you doing? You look good."

Patrisse rolled her eyes.

"You still tell lies, don't you, Jerold."

Jerold laughed and took her hand.

"Patrisse, Darcy and I are praying for you. I mentioned you at church last night. We're all praying."

"Isn't that something," she answered. "Jerold Volker, a praying man!"

Jerold laughed, but Patrisse wanted to talk.

"Jerold, thanks for your help financially with all of this. I was so worried about how I or Darrion would be able to pay."

Jerold waved his hand.

"Don't mention it. It's taken care of. I told Janice about it, and she agreed right away. You don't have anything to worry about; the foundation will cover what we can't."

Patrisse closed her eyes for a moment and Jerold thought she had fallen asleep. She opened them suddenly.

"Jerold," she said weakly, "I'm getting tired and need to rest, but I have one more thing I need to ask you."

Jerold sat down in the chair next to the bed and squeezed her hand.

"Okay," he said, "what can I do?"

"I don't know how to ask this, but I think I'll just come right out with it. Jerold, when I'm gone, I'd like it if you and Darcy could take Darrion."

Jerold was speechless.

Patrisse continued, "I know that's a lot to ask, and if you don't want to or can't, then I'll understand. I just don't know where he'll go. He loves you and Darcy. I've always believed you were special to him. I knew it. I know it's a shock, Jerold, but I don't have much time. Will you think about it? Talk to Darcy."

Jerold bowed his head. He thought about another little boy who had lost his mother. He knew how that felt. He saw his own seven-year-old eyes. This was a chance to help; this was a chance to get it right. After a second or two, he looked into Patrisse's eyes.

"Patrisse, I don't need a lot of time. I know Darcy, too. We'll do it. I'll take him in and when we're married, he'll stay with us."

Patrisse closed her eyes and Jerold left the room. He spoke to Darcy that night and she agreed that he had done the right thing. The next morning, Patrisse woke up in heaven. The funeral took place a few days later on a cold, snowy day. Jerold still remembered that very well. Darrion had done all right, considering everything that had happened. There was a time of grieving, but Patrisse had done well preparing him for what was to come. Like his mother, he was strong.

$ $ $

Jerold and Darcy were married just a couple of months later, and Darrion was one of the groomsmen. They lit a candle at the wedding in honor of Patrisse. Jerold knew that she would be especially happy.

Now Jerold noticed Darrion coming out of the bathroom, looking sharp in his navy blue suit and red tie.

"Do I look okay?" he asked Jerold.

"You look great," Jerold replied.

At that moment Darcy emerged from the ladies' room.

"Well, gentlemen," she said, "let's go. We don't want to be late for the judge."

The three of them walked into family courtroom number eight, where they would meet the Honorable Judge Henry B. Walker. Jerold had arranged for his attorney, Jay Schmidt, to handle the case and he was in the courtroom already.

"Good morning," Jay told them as they entered. "Have a seat here at the table. The paperwork has already been completed. The judge will call you to the front. It shouldn't take very long."

Jerold smiled and Darcy took Darrion's hand.

"It's going to be okay," she told him.

In a few minutes the judge entered the courtroom and everyone stood. He told them to be seated and then he took the papers before him and began to read them. He looked serious as he peered over his reading glasses. After a few minutes, he called Jerold, Darcy and Darrion to the bench.

"Mr. and Mrs. Volker," he began, "the paperwork is in order. There doesn't seem to be any issue or problem preventing this adoption from happening today."

"No sir, your honor. We're ready."

"Darrion," the judge said, looking through his glasses at him, "do you understand what is happening today? If I approve this, then you will officially be a part of the Volker family. You will live with them and have their name. I want to know today, before I sign off, is this what you want?"

Darrion cleared his throat and looked right at the judge.

"Yes sir," he said, "I do."

"Good," Judge Walker, "I am glad. Then it's a done deal."

The judge signed the paper and handed copies to Jay Schmidt and to the clerk.

"Congratulations to all of you," he said.

Darrion hugged Darcy while Jerold put his hand on Darrion's shoulder.

"We're family now," he told the youth. "It's what

your mom wanted and we do, too."

"I know," Darrion replied. "Thanks."

∮ ∮ ∮

The winter weather gave way to spring, and the Reds were back at the ball park by the river. Cincinnati fans were dreaming of the World Series. A developer had made the headlines by proposing a new type of shopping/entertainment complex on the river front. Local politicians were lining up on both sides of the issue. Change was in the air.

Change was also real for the new Volker family. Jerold had been talking regularly to Janice. They had a lot of catching up to do, but it was more than that. Janice had a proposition for Jerold. When Jerold heard it, he was skeptical, but she urged him to talk to Darcy, who thought the idea was wonderful for them and for Darrion. Jerold had to admit, it did appeal to him.

∮ ∮ ∮

On a warm Wednesday morning Jerold Volker, successful vice-president, went into the office of Derek Lonaker and tendered his resignation. It was shocking news that spread quickly throughout the bank. No one could believe that Volker was giving up that great position to move to a little town in Kentucky and run a two-bit bank. There had to be more to the story, they thought. There wasn't and, then again, there was. At first Derek Lonaker tried to persuade Jerold to reconsider. After some lengthy discussions, though, he relented.

On Jerold's last day, a big farewell party was given

in his honor. Everyone throughout the building came to say good-bye and enjoy cake, punch and a few sandwiches. Associates from all over the building came to wish Jerold well, and it was obvious that some were also angling for his old job. Jerold spent the better part of an hour talking to different folks, some of whom he barely knew. Toward the end of the party, Ed and Jason approached.

"Mr. Volker," Ed said, "we just wanted to stop by to congratulate you. I want you to know I'm really proud of you. You're going to do great."

"Thanks, Ed," Jerold replied. "You know, I'm really going to miss you. Every day you saw me into this building and every day you let me out to go home."

"That's right," Jason said, putting down his third piece of cake, "It's just not going to be the same without you."

Jerold realized that, for the years he had been here, he had taken these guys for granted, as he had many things. He embraced both of them.

"I'm the one who's losing out," he said. "You guys are the best. Keep up the good work and don't worry. We'll be back to visit. If the Reds get into the Series, then we'll all go, on me."

They all laughed and Ed and Jason walked away. Jerold watched them leave with a lump in his throat.

The party wound down around five o'clock. Jerold found himself standing by the punch bowl, alone. He looked around the room. It was a mess; his co-workers certainly knew how to party. He thought about his years here, and all the people he didn't really know or take the time to know. There were a few who had really worked to get to know him: Ed, Jason and a handful of others. Then he thought of Patrisse.

"Well, Patrisse," Jerold said aloud, though there was no one there to hear, "I guess it's time for me to go. I want you to know how much I appreciated all you did. You saw me when no one else could, and I'll never forget that. I want you to know, too, that we're going to raise Darrion to be the man you envisioned. You'll be proud... Oh, yeah, Patrisse, I know where you are you'll see a fellow, a carpenter. He might be wearing a gray shirt and red cap. When you see him tell him Jerold says 'hey.' Will you do that? Thanks."

With that, Jerold Volker made one final trip to the basement garage and drove the BMW out and down I-75. He was going home.

Chapter Twelve

The Volker family left Cincinnati early Saturday morning, Jerold and Darrion in the rented truck and Darcy in the BMW. They had been packed for almost a week. The drive to Pikesville didn't seem as long as it had the first time. Darrion had never been there, so he was full of questions. He wanted to know about the school and football. Jerold spent nearly an hour just answering.

They pulled into Pikesville just a little before ten in the morning and drove down Main Street to Cambridge. They turned and drove to 203 Cambridge, where a van was already in the drive. As Jerold parked the truck in front of the house, he and Darrion heard a scream. In seconds the front door of the house flew open and Martha Ruth came dashing out.

"They're here!" she exclaimed. "They're here!"

She ran to Darcy, who was just getting out of the BMW; and her brother, Joey, ran to Jerold and Darrion, who were standing at the back of the truck.

"Hi," he called out. "You guys are early. Mom and

Dad aren't quite ready."

Jerold was puzzled. What did he mean, "Not quite ready?" Seconds later Tony appeared from behind the house. It was obvious he had been working. As Jerold looked around, he could see that Tony had been working a lot. The walls around the driveway were repaired. The windows were no longer blackened and burned.

"Hey," he called out to Tony, "I thought we were going to work on this together."

Tony shrugged.

"Well," he said, "once your sister gets something going, there's no stopping her."

At that moment, Janice came out of the front door.

"Hey," she called out, "how are you all?"

She ran down the front steps to hug Darcy.

"And this must be Darrion," she said as she put her hand on his shoulder.

"Yes, ma'am," Darrion replied.

Janice smiled widely.

"You don't have to call me ma'am, Darrion," she said. "Call me Aunt Jan."

Joey worked his way to the front of the group.

"I'm Joey," he said, reaching out his hand to Darrion. "Do you like football?"

Darrion's eyes lit up.

"Do I like football?" he exclaimed. "You bet I do!"

"Awesome," Joey replied. "Let's go to the backyard."

"Wait a minute," Tony interrupted. "There will be time for that. First, though, we've got to get unloaded. We need your help."

"Dad," Martha Ruth said, "can we show Darrion his surprise first?"

Darrion's eyes lit up again.

Janice answered, "I think we should. Come on in the house, everyone."

Jerold, Darcy and Darrion walked into the house, their house. Jerold was amazed at how much it had changed since he had been there last. Tony was right. Once Janice started working, she was unstoppable.

"Come right this way," Martha Ruth told them as she led Darrion by the hand.

They walked down the hallway to the last bedroom. Jerold recognized it right away: his old bedroom.

"Okay, Darrion," Martha Ruth said, "Close your eyes."

Darrion closed his eyes and Martha Ruth flung open the door. Inside, Jerold could see that the room had been painted blue. The curtains had all the logos of the NFL. The bedspread matched the curtains and there were football posters on the wall, too. In the center of the bed, right between the pillows, was a teddy bear dressed in a Bengals' jersey.

"I had that one made special," Janice told Jerold.

Darrion was speechless. It was incredible, like a dream.

"Thank you," he said, "thank you."

Martha Ruth put her hand on his arm and Joey spoke.

"That's okay," he said. "That's what families do."

Jerold, Darcy, Tony, Janice and the kids helped unload the truck. They began moving boxes around and setting things up. Jerold was shocked that they were getting to stay in the house that night.

"That was Janice's idea," Tony told him. "She insisted on it."

Later that night, Jerold walked down the hall and pushed open the door of his old bedroom, now Darrion's. He looked in at him sleeping soundly, his hand resting on the bear, then, walked back to the room that had once belonged to his parents. Darcy was already in bed.

"Welcome home, Mr. Volker," she said as he climbed into bed.

"You know, Darce, this feels real good. I think we can be here for a long time."

"I hope so," Darcy said. "I want to raise our children here."

Jerold sat up.

"Children," he said. "Uh, Darce, we've only got one."

Darcy smiled.

"That's true," she said, "for about another six months. Congratulations, Dad. Darrion's gonna have a brother or sister."

Jerold hugged her, realizing he'd never been happier. There was plenty of room in his heart.

Photo courtesy of TeAnne Chartrau

About the Author

Bill Thomas lives in Washington, Missouri. He is an "at-risk" teacher in the Union, MO public school system, and also teaches online for Dallas Christian College. He served for 11 years as the preaching minister at Stony Point Christian Church in Kansas City, KS. He has also worked for 10 years as a Youth and Education minister. *From the Ashes* is his first novel.